WHERE
TRUTH
LIES

HEATHER DAWN GRAY

Cover photo/layout credits to Stephen
Ewashko and Romi Burianova

DEDICATION

To my husband Ron, and our daughters, Colby and Sabra, who hold my heart.

ACKNOWLEDGMENTS

I am so grateful to the many people who have read my first book, *The Lie*. Your support and encouragement. gave me the confidence to continue with this sequel.

In writing *Where Truth Lies*, I relied heavily on many people to read my draft and, provide honest feedback. Of particular mention, and in no particular order, my indebted gratitude goes to David, Debbie, Mike, Nick, Colby, Ron, Christine, Lenore, Kim, Glen, Frank, Peter, Gary, and countless others.

Thanks to Stephen Ewashko, Romi Burianova, and Umid Mirsaidov for the professional cover. Umid, I couldn't have asked for a better Omar, you encapsulated him impeccably, Stephen, with assistance from Romi, captured Umid just the way I had envisioned. Then, Stephen, you designed the cover, to align with the prequel perfectly.

To Colby and Sabra, thank you for always encouraging me to become better versions of myself.

Ron, I couldn't ask for better support. You ensure that while I write, we can eat. You lift me up when I'm down, steady me when I stumble, and applaud me when I soar. You are my everything.

CHAPTER ONE

Brie stiffened under Omar's arm. He pulled her in tighter and smiled. She stared straight ahead. She'd acquiesce. That's one thing he liked about her; he could always convince her to give in. Even if she didn't understand, he needed her to play along just the same.

"There are propane heaters. It'll be cozy. Might be our last chance to sit outside before it gets too cold." Omar hoped to soften the tension. They needed to dine on the patio.

"All right. But if it's too cold we're moving inside." Brie flipped her long brown hair forward over her shoulder.

Omar bent down and kissed her on the forehead, relieved.

Under his protective arm, she shivered as they stepped outside. *Everyone better be ready. This needs to go off without a hitch.*

The hostess showed them to the table, prearranged by Omar; nearest the corner where the two sidewalks met. Omar pulled out Brie's chair for her and slid it in before sitting in the chair across from her. He rubbed his hands together and blew into his cupped palms.

"See I'm not the only one who's cold. This is ridiculous Omar, let's go inside." Brie slid her chair back.

Damn I should have controlled that. He reached across the table for her hand. "Let's just give it a few more minutes. I'm sure we'll get used to it."

Brie rolled her eyes and sighed, picking up the menu.

A waitress appeared at the side of the table and moved the portable heater closer. "Is that better? Perhaps a drink would help warm you up?"

"Want to share a bottle of Malbec?"

Brie cocked her head. "Since when do you like red wine?"

"Oh, just thought I'd give it a go, maybe it'll warm me up." Omar nodded at the waitress. "A bottle of your best Malbec, please."

Brie sighed. "Why do you always think it needs to be the best?"

Omar clasped his hands beneath the table. "Why not? I can afford it. Is it wrong that I want to treat you special?"

"No, but you don't need to spend lots of money to do that."

He unclasped his hands and placed one hand on hers. "I know Brie. But you are special and I want to do everything I can for you. Is that so wrong?"

Brie's shoulders relaxed, and a smile hinted at the corners of her mouth. "You exasperate me sometimes Omar."

His thumb traced the back of her hand. "I'm starving. Want to share an appetizer?"

The waitress returned with the wine and Omar pointed to Brie. "She's the wine connoisseur."

As if on cue, the commotion came from both directions at once. Brie sipped the wine and smiled at the waitress, giving her permission to pour more. She hadn't noticed the distraction. Omar leaned back in his chair, smiling. Finally, she strained to see where the singing came from as the two groups entered their sight lines.

Brie's head snapped back to Omar. The excitement seemed to drain from her face as she realized what was happening. In no time the crowd stood in front of them, pointing at Brie and singing the line Bruno Mars made famous, *I think I want to marry you.* She turned away from the crowd in time to see Omar kneel, reach into his pocket and pull out a small white box.

The singing stopped. His hand trembled as he lifted the lid and gazed into her eyes. "Brie, I don't just think, I know I want to marry you. Will you marry me?"

Brie stared down; eyes wide. Not the reaction he hoped for. There were no tears or smiles or nods. She glanced up at the crowd and scanned the patio. Then the doors from the restaurant burst open and invited friends spilled out with whoops of congratulations. Omar ignored the panic in Brie's eyes. He grabbed her left hand and slid the ring on. She still hadn't said yes, but she didn't stop him from sliding the ring on either. A half-hearted smile crossed her lips and he leaned in for a kiss. She didn't kiss him back, but he dismissed it. They'd been arguing before the proposal. She'd come around. Especially with everyone there to celebrate. Brie relented and accepted the hugs and words of congratulations. *Yep, she'd come around.*

His pocket vibrated and he pulled out his phone. 'Mom' appeared on the screen. He slid the notifications off. He'd tell her all about it in the morning. She'd been on his case for ten years to get married and start a family; she'd almost lost hope.

Omar wiped his forehead, relieved to no longer keep secrets. This almost went badly. The fact she hadn't said yes weighed on him, but she'd get over her tiff and after a night of celebration tell him how happy she is.

***

The sun warmed Omar awake. Even before the fog lifted from his thoughts, he felt the niggle of something good. Then it hit him. He asked Brie to marry him. The details were hazy, but it seemed everyone, including Brie, had a good time. He rolled over to relish at the sight of her lying next to him. But the comforter was tossed aside and her nest of pillows was empty. His eyes closed and his arm swung over his face to shield sensitive eyes from the sunlight. The vestiges of a hangover pounded in his temples. Brie would often get up before him and make a big breakfast. Bile rose in his throat and his stomach turned over. Besides not hearing her in the kitchen, he couldn't smell anything cooking. He relaxed back into the pillows and sighed, grateful for the solitude; the turning of his stomach subsided. He ran his left hand across the nightstand till it found the phone hanging over the edge. *What time is it?* He cracked open his eyes, shielding them with his other hand. But the time didn't register. Instead notifications for nine voicemails from his mother caused him to sit up, a little too suddenly. He pushed the voicemail button.

"Omar, this is Mom. Dad's on the way to the hospital. I called an ambulance. He just collapsed in pain. Call me back."

Omar's upset stomach rose to the back of his throat. He clicked on the next message.

"Omar, Mom again. Please call me back. It's serious."

He didn't bother listening to the rest of the messages.

"Brie, Brie," he called out as he swung his legs over the side of the bed and rushed to the kitchen. "Have you heard from Mom?"

But his voice landed on granite countertops, stainless steel appliances and hardwood floors, creating a hollow echo. He touched his phone to redial the last number. His mom answered on the first ring.

"Omar. Where have you been? I've been trying to get you all night."

Not wanting this to be the way he announced his engagement, he mumbled, "Ah I got together with friends. What hospital are you at? Is Dad okay?"

His dad complained of the flu the other day, and his complexion had a grey tinge, but it didn't seem serious.

"We're at Mount Sinai hospital. And no, he's not okay. He's on pain meds which help him sleep. There's a problem with his kidneys."

Kidneys? What could have caused this?

He scanned the apartment for a sign of Brie and noticed a note on the kitchen counter. Grabbing it, he headed back to the bedroom to get ready.

"On my way." He threw his phone and the note on the bathroom counter and turned on the shower.

CHAPTER TWO

Omar dropped into a chair in the corner of the room nearest the window, resting his head in his hands, the cold metal arms biting into his elbows. Pounding temples reminded him he should have popped some Advil before rushing out the door and he wished he'd grabbed something to sop up the acid in his stomach. But he promised his mom if she went home to sleep, he wouldn't leave his father's side, so he sat back in the chair, committed to suffering out his hangover. And, he reasoned, he deserved this pain after ignoring his mother's calls the previous night.

The thin blue blanket highlighted his dad's grey skin and shallow breaths. At least he didn't appear to be in pain and rested with the help of medication. The wires and tubes connected him to machines tapping out a hypnotic calming rhythm.

Omar took Brie's note out of his pocket and reread it.

Omar,

I woke up this morning and realized I needed to put some distance between us. Your proposal last night, while romantic, was very unexpected and I have to think about it. I love you, but I'm not sure I'm ready for this. I've taken next week off work and am driving to Boston to spend time with my sister. I hope you understand.

Love Brie

The initial reaction to the note left a small indent in the bathroom wall and a throbbing big toe. How had he misread her? Most women would be ecstatic with a proposal like the one he put together. What other response was there to expect but yes? After living together for over a year he thought he knew her. And she just sold her own condo. Why wasn't she ready for marriage?

Omar rubbed his eyes and ran a hand through his hair, leaning back to rest his head on the wall behind him. How quickly things change; from what he expected would be the best night of his life to a nightmare.

Footsteps intermingled with voices approached the room. The partially closed door swung open and a group of white coats entered. A tall man, barely older than Omar crossed the floor with hand extended.

"I'm Dr. Berenstein and these people behind me are medical students. You are…"

Omar stood up and grasped the doctor's hand, cold and smooth to the touch. "I'm Omar, Didar's son. My mom just left. She'll be sorry to have missed you."

The doctor waved toward the door. "We're just going to examine your father. Can I get you to step outside for a minute? When we're done, we'll talk to you about what we think is going on here."

Omar retreated to the hall and paced till the door reopened and a student invited him back in. His dad remained asleep.

The cloud of white coats parted and Dr. Berenstein moved toward Omar. He reached out and patted Omar's shoulder. "I'm afraid the news is not good Omar. Your dad is in acute renal failure caused by a bacterial infection in his blood. Usually kidneys will recover from this, but it doesn't look good. The IV antibiotics are taking care of the infection, but the kidneys don't appear to be bouncing back. We'll keep him drugged and resting to give him the best chance of gaining strength. If his kidneys don't recover, he'll need dialysis and eventually a kidney transplant."

Omar's head spun and his knees weakened. He heard Dr. Berenstein bark out an order for someone to pull the chair closer and he felt himself being supported until the seat slid under his thighs. The room went black.

"Just keep your head down for a few minutes. You'll be fine. Has this ever happened to you before?"

Thoughts swirled in his pounding head. The smell of bleach and bodily fluids permeated his senses. The fog lifted as he realized he sat in his dad's hospital room with his head between his knees and the green he stared at was the floor. And then he realized he'd fainted. What kind of man faints over hearing his father is ill? Thankful he didn't have to look at them as he stared at the floor, he let out a chuckle. "I'm afraid I partied a bit too hard last night. I guess it's all too much for me. No, this has never happened before."

He straightened up and a nurse slapped on a blood pressure cuff.

"Perhaps we can talk about this another time." Dr. Berenstein made his way back toward the door.

"No, please Dr. Berenstein, what is the prognosis?" Omar leaned forward, the nurse placed a hand on his shoulder, preventing him from standing. "If his kidneys fail and he needs dialysis, how long can he survive?"

"I think we're getting ahead of ourselves here. We still hope his kidneys may recover. There are options for home dialysis which makes things much easier these days. If the kidneys fail, however, he'll need a kidney transplant. But again, that's a conversation for another day. Let him rest and we'll see how much kidney function he has in a day or two." Dr. Berenstein turned back toward the door.

"Just one more thing before you go. What are the criteria for being a kidney donor?"

Without turning Dr. Berenstein paused. "Again, we'll talk about that another day. Right now, I need to move on to the next patient."

The footsteps of Dr. Berenstein and his entourage receded down the hallway.

The nurse removed the blood pressure cuff and gave Omar a squeeze on the shoulder. "Blood pressure's fine. I suggest you go find some food and drink some water. Your dad will be okay while you're gone. You need to look after yourself if you're going to take care of him."

There was judgement in her eyes, despite her smile. Omar wanted to tell her he wasn't an alcoholic; he'd been celebrating his engagement. But he nodded and shuffled out of the room, down the hall to the elevators.

In the cafeteria, with a sandwich in front of him, he summoned the courage to text Brie. He explained his dad's situation and apologized for not realizing she wasn't ready for marriage. Then he tucked his pride aside and begged her to come back. He needed her support right now.

On his second glass of water, her text came back.

> *I've pulled onto the shoulder for a minute. I'm so sorry about your dad. I'll take the next exit off the freeway and turn around. I should be there in about three hours.*

Omar breathed a sigh of relief. Why he felt better, he couldn't say; perhaps the water or the sandwich or knowing Brie decided to come back.

He'd focus on saving his dad. In fact, he'd donate his own kidney if it came to that.

The engagement no longer seemed important.

CHAPTER THREE

Omar woke with a start. The hard plastic of the short-backed chair offered no head support and pain radiated from his neck down his shoulder. Through the dimly lit hospital room, the curtains around his dad's bed came into focus behind Brie's tear-filled eyes staring down at him. He rose unsteadily, and she reached out, wrapped her arms around his waist and buried her face in his chest. A shudder escaped, but he stopped short of breaking down. He wouldn't lose control.

"I'm so sorry, Omar. I know how close you are to your dad. This is so difficult."

Omar took a deep breath and closed his eyes, holding her tightly.

"What a nightmare, Brie. His kidneys may never recover. For now, they're letting him rest. In a day or two, they'll reassess. I've already decided that if he needs a kidney, I'll be the donor."

Brie pushed away, searching Omar's eyes.

"I can understand how you want to donate, but are you a match? How much of a risk is this to you?"

Omar released Brie from his arms and motioned for her to sit in the vacated chair. He perched himself on the window ledge.

"I've googled it and the first criteria is to be the same blood type. I don't know what blood type Dad is, but I plan to find out. If we pass this first hurdle, there'll be further testing, but children of a parent have good odds of being able to donate."

Omar turned to his father. Didar wasn't a large man to begin with, but lying in that hospital bed he seemed so small. His eyelids fluttered and Omar held his breath.

"It's okay Dad, rest."

Didar settled back down, the only motion visible the rise and fall of his chest.

"I can understand your desire to donate, but what if something happens to one of your kidneys? There's no one who can donate to you."

Brie reached across and stroked his knee.

"Maybe one day I'll have children too. I hope my family tree doesn't end with me. And besides the doctor said he has an infection. That doesn't sound like a hereditary thing to me."

Brie shrunk back in the chair; her gaze shifted to the floor. Omar hadn't meant to sound like he expected a future involving marriage and children.

"I'm sorry Brie. I didn't mean it the way it sounded. Can we forget about the engagement right now?"

Brie opened her purse and unzipped an inside pocket, pulling out the ring and offered it to Omar. "I didn't say yes, and I don't know if I can. I know you've been working on your anger outbursts, but I've seen a few over the past little while. I'm just not sure I'm ready to jump in until I'm sure you have a handle on your temper. Hang on to it until I'm ready."

Omar grasped her hand and closed her fingers around the ring. "Keep it until you see how serious I am about putting things into perspective. I can control my temper and I will. You don't have to wear the ring. In fact, maybe it's better if you don't. Mom would plan the wedding within minutes of seeing it. In fact, she probably already has it planned, and is just waiting to see a glimmer of hope we might think about it."

Brie smiled as she tucked the ring back into her purse.

"So, they don't know about last night?"

"No, I waited to tell them together. They adore you and I wanted you to see their faces too."

Brie's smile vanished and she lowered her gaze. "Sorry, I'm just not ready."

"No, no, it's okay. I'm the one who's sorry for not being more diligent about my outbursts. And now with everything, it's not a good time anyway. I promise I'll show you that I'm someone you can count on to keep a cool head in all situations." Omar's eyes filled with tears and he cleared his throat. "Thanks for coming back. I need your support."

Brie rose and sat next to him on the ledge.

"I'll be here," she whispered as she slid her arm around his waist.

The nurse who had taken his blood pressure marched into the room to check Didar's vitals.

"Glad to see you have someone to take care of you." A smile lit her face, and she winked at them.

Omar blushed and Brie's brows knit as she searched his face for answers. Before she had a chance to say anything, Omar jumped up and stepped closer to the nurse. "Is my dad's blood type recorded in his chart?"

"Yes, we had him typed in case he needed to go to surgery. Why?"

"Oh, I'm just thinking ahead." Omar's hands pushed deep into his pants pockets. Why did this nurse have so much power over him? When she walked into the room, he felt twelve years old. "I've decided to donate my kidney if Dad needs it."

The nurse stopped and turned to Omar. Her voice soft. "Your parents raised a good man. What's your blood type?"

Omar retrieved his wallet from his back pocket, pulled out his blood donor card and handed it to her. "I'm B Positive."

The nurse glanced at the card and passed it back. "Now I shouldn't say this, patient confidentiality and all, but you're not eligible to donate. Didar's type is O Positive and can only receive donations from compatible O positive or O negative donors."

Omar returned the card to his wallet and slumped back down beside Brie. Could this day get any worse? He felt helpless before, but now he was completely useless.

The nurse patted his knee on her way out of the room.

"Now what?" Omar searched Brie's eyes for an answer.

"Don't get ahead of yourself. We don't know if he'll need a kidney, so don't go there."

"But I'm an only child and Dad's only brother died years ago. There's no other relative that can step up."

Brie's eyes brightened, and she nudged Omar's side. "But there is another sibling. Remember you matched to someone on MyGeneticFamily? Didn't you say you had a half-sister?"

A million thoughts exploded in Omar's brain. Jahana might be the answer. He'd reached out to her when he first matched, but when she didn't respond, he hadn't pursued it. He realized it might be uncomfortable for his parents. But things were different now.

"Brie, I would've thought about it eventually, but yes, I have a half sibling. How can she ignore me when she finds out it might be a matter of life and death?"

Brie smiled. Omar rubbed her knee. *We're meant to be together. Can you see that too?*

CHAPTER FOUR

His dad held his hand as they crossed the street. The lights cast a glow matching the satisfaction sitting in the pit of his stomach. He wore his new boots and smiled with satisfaction, their clomp on the pavement sounded like horse hooves.

"Hurry Omar, cars are coming." His dad's grip tightened

Omar picked up the pace and hopped onto the sidewalk on the other side, stomping his feet for extra effect. He looked down at his boots, admiring their buckles, when his dad stopped abruptly and the glow inside his tummy turned dark. A big, smelly man with a scary low voice stood in front of them.

His dad shook the man's hand. "Hey, how's it going?"

Omar took a step back, but not far enough to lose his grip. He strained to hear the man's response.

"Down on my luck, not going too well." He turned his head and coughed loudly, spitting into the grass behind him. "Lost my job two months ago and now I've got this cough that won't go away."

The stranger never raised his eyes. Omar squirmed and tugged on his dad's hand. His heart raced. What if this man got angry? He was way bigger than his dad. He tugged again; this time harder.

But his dad remained planted in front of the stranger, continuing to carry on a conversation. Omar no longer cared what they talked about, he just wanted to move on. They'd be late and he'd been looking forward to seeing *Toy Story* for the last week. His dad got tickets to the first showing. Now he was at risk of missing it. He pulled again. This time his dad turned to him, the creases in his forehead visible.

"One minute, Omar. I'm talking with this gentleman." Didar turned back to the stranger.

Nothing about this person is a gentleman. But Omar knew better than to push his dad further, so he stood quietly, counting seconds in his head and peering up at the big man periodically, then looking down at his boots. His tummy hurt.

He was at one hundred and two when his dad let go of his hand and took a step forward. Omar stared up into the man's face, it looked angry. Was his dad about to fight a man twice his size? It wasn't a fight he could win. But then his dad slid his hand into his jacket pocket and pulled out his wallet. He handed several bills to the man who looked back with tear brimmed eyes. The wind stirred and Omar shivered. He pulled up his collar and shoved his hands in his pockets. His mother called it his good jacket. One he only wore on special occasions. Small snowflakes appeared on his sleeves and he watched them disappear into tiny droplets.

The man whispered something and Omar again peeked around his father. Tears streamed down the stranger's face. Omar lifted his gaze and stared straight into his father's eyes looking down at him. His eyes sparkled. He patted Omar on the head and reached for his hand, turning away from the stranger and continuing down the street. Omar hip-hopped to keep up. Was his dad hurrying to get away from the man, or hurrying to get to the theatre on time? His hip-hops turned into a jog.

The buttery goodness of popcorn greeted him as his dad pushed open the heavy door. His tummy grumbled. The sick feeling left back on the street with the strange man.

The line for tickets was short and Omar bounced up and down when they waited for popcorn, the buckles on his boots reflecting the marquis lights.

Omar reached into the bag of popcorn perched between them, stuffing the handful into his mouth and wiggling his bottom back into the slippery red seat, his new boots on display straight out in front of him. He chewed, then swallowed before turning to his dad. "Did you know that man on the street?"

Omar reached into the popcorn bag and pulled out another large handful. His dad paid for extra butter and the top layer always tasted best. A few stray kernels bounced off his lap and onto the floor. He reached in and grabbed another handful. For some reason it was acceptable to eat like this in a theatre, but not at home.

"No Omar, I've never seen him before."

Didar also reached into the bag, taking a few kernels and popping them into his mouth. Omar took note, wishing he had better manners like his dad. The salt tasted like the ocean and he licked his lips hungrily. It was too good to only eat a few kernels at a time.

He swallowed his mouthful and peered up at his dad. "Why did you stop and talk to him? And why did you give him money?"

Didar wiped his mouth with his napkin. "You'll learn in your lifetime Omar; some people have bad luck. No matter how hard they try, they can't get ahead. And those of us who are better off and have had better luck, can help them out."

Omar brightened. "Oh, I've heard of this. It's called paying it forward, right Dad?"

Didar smiled at his son. "Some people call it that, but in my case, I call it paying it backward."

Omar squinted and wrinkled his nose trying to figure out what that meant. But then his dad continued.

"As a young man, I didn't realize how lucky I was. I took advantage of people for many years and never helped others. In fact, some might say I hurt others. I was a grown man before I realized the error of my ways. Thanks to your mother I see things more clearly. So now when I help others, I'm paying for the things I've done wrong in my life."

The cloudy, far off look in his dad's eyes bothered Omar. "So, you help others now so you feel better about not helping them before?" It didn't quite make sense to Omar.

"I guess so. But I'm hopeful God knows I've changed and my good deeds will atone for the bad things I've done in my life."

Omar didn't understand what atone meant, but the movie was about to start and he didn't want to keep talking about bad things. In his eyes his dad could do no wrong and couldn't imagine what he needed to make up for.

Didar patted Omar's shoulder. "I hope you'll never have a reason to right wrongs in your life."

Omar's eyes widened. Was it too late? Maybe he'd already done bad things he needed to pay for.

Before the trailers started, his dad leaned over and whispered in his ear. "You're a good boy; try to remember to pay it forward every chance you get."

CHAPTER FIVE

The computer screen glowed in the darkened room. Omar slouched in bed propped up with pillows, a laptop resting against his thighs. He yawned and ran a palm through his hair. Heavy eyes teased him; every time he closed them the full reality of his dad's situation sank in and he couldn't fall asleep.

Be positive.

A Google search showed the waiting list for a kidney stretched beyond five years. Would his dad last that long? He had no choice but to reach out to the half-sister he'd never met. How would he find the words to convince her to donate a kidney to a father she didn't know? He opened the MyGeneticFamily message centre and started typing.

Jahana

Please don't close this message before reading it to the end. I reached out last year when you matched as a sister to me. I'm not sure if this is a paternal or maternal relationship, but I suspect we're related through my dad. Do you know? I've never received a response from you, but I'm contacting you again because of a life or death situation.

My father recently went into kidney failure. I wanted to donate my kidney, but my blood type is incompatible with his, he's O Positive so needs an O donor. This is a big ask, but I'm wondering what your blood type is? And whether you know if we have a common father or a common mother. I'm desperate to find a kidney for my dad. His one sibling died years ago in Iran, executed by the regime. I was an only child until I matched with you, so it appears there are no other living relatives that might match to him. The waiting list for a kidney is over five years. I can't imagine he would last that long on dialysis.

I've never told my parents about you. He's been a good dad to me. If he's your father and knew of your existence, I'm sure he would have contacted you. I respected your privacy when you didn't respond, but I need your help.

Can you please reply so we can set up a time to talk about this? From your profile it appears you live in Ottawa. I'm in New York City. Perhaps we could start by talking over the phone. Please respond.

Your brother,

Omar

Omar read and re-read the message before sending. Did it have the right tone? Too pushy? Did it compel her to respond without scaring her away? He clicked the send button.

He slid the laptop onto the other side of the bed and rested his outstretched hand on Brie's pillows. She decided it best to stay with a friend until she worked through her feelings. When would she return? He needed her. He rotated his neck forward and side to side trying to work the stiffness out from falling asleep in the hospital room chair. He needed to shut out the last twenty-four hours or he'd never fall asleep. He pulled up the covers and closed his eyes.

The phone rang, waking Omar from a nightmare. His heart raced and he fumbled to retrieve the phone off his nightstand. 'Mom' appeared on the screen. He sat bolt upright.

"Mom is everything okay?"

"Yes, yes, everything's fine. Sorry to wake you. The nurses say the doctor makes rounds in about an hour. Can you be here when he comes by?"

Omar ran a hand across his eyes and sunk back down into his pillows, his heart still racing and pounding in his temples. His mother's request slowly working into legible sentences.

"Omar, are you still there?"

He grabbed one of Brie's pillows and slid it behind his head, trying to elevate himself to consciousness.

"Yeah Mom, I'll be there. Any change with Dad?"

Omar swung his legs over the side of the bed and put his phone on speaker as he staggered into the bathroom.

"He's had a restful night, but seems to be moving around more. I think they reduced his pain meds, so he's more aware."

Omar hesitated in front of the toilet, shifting his weight from side to side. He couldn't pee with his mom listening.

"Mom, I'll be there in half an hour. See you soon."

As he hung up, he noticed a message from MyGeneticFamily pop up on the screen. He sat on the toilet and opened it. Fingers trembled as he clicked on the link.

Hello Omar,

I didn't respond when you first reached out because I don't want to pursue a relationship with your father. Yes, I'm confident your father is the link between us. I've recently learned I was adopted and I've tracked down my mother. She only has one other daughter. I haven't found my father.

I can't imagine how difficult it must be to find out your dad is in kidney failure.

My blood type is O Positive so I pass the first test, but I won't be donating a kidney. I call him your dad, because for reasons I would rather not discuss I don't consider him to be my father.

I can offer you one avenue to try. There's a site called GENmatch. They don't test your DNA, but take DNA results people enter and compare them on a public forum. This gives you an opportunity to see if there are matches to your DNA with people who had their DNA tested on sites other than MyGeneticFamily.

As you said, in your first message, your dad was a "real lady's man", so perhaps there are other siblings out there that may help him out. Again, I'm sorry, but I won't donate my kidney.

Jahana

"Damn it!" He threw the phone at the vanity, and it bounced back at him. He clenched and unclenched his jaw running his hand through his hair. Omar recognized the anger burst. It happened less frequently, but it still happened and if he didn't get it under control, he'd never get Brie to agree to marry him.

Responding now would make matters worse. He rose and flushed, then stepped into the shower, letting the cool water wake him and dissipate the anger. The coconut fragrance of the shampoo permeated his nostrils. The rise and fall of his chest slowed. Facing into the water, he allowed himself a minute to simply exist before hopping out and towelling off. Ten minutes later he was in the car and on his way to the hospital.

****

Didar lay in bed staring at the faces surrounding him. His heart quickened and sweat formed on his palms. Mahtob's eyes belied her smile, flitting from him to the window and back again. And Omar stood back, somber, fidgeting. Strangers in white coats lined the other side of the bed and around the foot. A rhythmic beeping matched flashing lights on the IV pole to his right.

"Do you know where you are?" A deep voice projected from the foot of the bed.

Didar lowered his chin to identify the speaker. "I assume a hospital." Didar's voice cracked, and he coughed. How could he sound confident when nothing made sense? The kitchen. Mahtob. Freezing cold. The smell of roast beef cooking. *How did I end up in a hospital bed?*

"Correct, you're in the hospital. I'm Dr. Berenstein and the others are medical students and residents." A wide sweeping gesture included the men and women standing around Didar's bed. "What day it is?"

Didar paused. *The backyard was full of leaves.* He closed his eyes. Why was it so difficult to concentrate? *He was going to rake leaves but he didn't feel well. Saturday was the day he did yard work.*

His eyes popped open. "Saturday?"

He noticed Mahtob glance at Omar. A tear travelled down her cheek.

The deep voice spoke up. "It's Monday. But I can understand why you might think it's still Saturday. You've been sedated since you arrived here Saturday evening."

"Why am I here?" Didar shifted his gaze to Omar. He couldn't wait any longer. Why wasn't anyone telling him what was going on? Mahtob stepped forward and stroked his cheek.

"You collapsed in the kitchen Didar. An infection in your blood has affected your kidneys."

He shifted his gaze to the doctor who murmured something to a student who left the room. Mahtob stroked his hand. Omar shifted his weight from one side to the other, looking like a bobble head at the end of the bed. Acid from his stomach rose to the back of his throat. He coughed. Mahtob handed him a glass of water with a straw.

Omar moved closer and squeezed his foot. "Dad, we'll get through this. We just need to find you a kidney. I looked into donating my own…"

Didar's eyes widened. "Kidney?" His eyes darted to the doctor. What's he talking about? You have my son donating a kidney to me?"

The doctor cleared his throat. "We're getting ahead of ourselves here."

Omar waved his hand in front of him. "Don't get upset Dad. My blood type isn't compatible. I can't donate. But I'll find someone who can."

Didar's stared back at the doctor.

"As for a kidney transplant, we have lots of time to discuss this. In the meantime, we'll put you on dialysis. The infection has damaged your kidneys, and they aren't recovering."

Didar stared at the doctor, not daring to glance at Mahtob. He clasped his hands under the sheet to control the trembling.

"We'll get you placed on the transplant registry too. Someone will be by with forms a little later today. You're in good health, Didar, so I expect you'll be okay. It's not dire. Let's not get too wrapped up in the logistics of things just yet. One step at a time." The doctor raised his eyebrows and looked directly at Omar. "He needs to rest and not worry." He returned his gaze to Didar. "Eventually you'll be able to do dialysis at home if you and your wife take the training. It's not as terrible as it used to be. Managing your condition until a kidney becomes available is possible. We'll talk more tomorrow."

And with that the white coat entourage left, taking everything but the awkward silence with them.

Didar cleared his throat. "Okay, you heard him. It's not as dire as it seems."

Mahtob wagged her finger at the two of them. "No more discussion about this. You heard the doctor. The best thing we can do right now is let you get some rest. I'm going home to do just that. Omar can you stay?"

Omar pulled out his phone and scrolled. "Yes, I've got two meetings but I'll reschedule for another day."

Didar opened his mouth to interrupt when Omar ushered Mahtob out the door and returned to his father's bed.

"Now Dad, don't worry about a thing. I have a plan. I'm sure we'll find a match and you won't have to wait years."

Didar stared at his son. So much hope in his eyes. He wanted to tell him not to worry. That he would overcome this somehow. But, how?

"What're your plans Omar? Where will you find a kidney for your old man?" Didar forced himself to smile.

"I've never told you this, but I paid for a DNA test through MyGeneticFamily last year. If I post the results on a website called GENmatch, perhaps I'll get lucky and find a match for you."

Didar struggled to sit up, eyes wide. "Omar, why would you do such a thing? You had a DNA test? Why?" He paused then continued. "What did you find out?"

Omar took a step back. His face bright red. "Why Dad? Why not? Maybe I'll find some relatives. I found…" But Omar stopped mid-sentence and shifted his attention to the weather outside, turning his back on Didar.

"Found what, Son? What exactly did you find?" Didar's face flushed and he bunched the sheets in a clenched fist.

Omar slowly turned and his face softened. "Nothing, Dad. Just a bunch of very distant cousins showed up as matches. Which is why I need to post my results on GENmatch. It'll spread the net and give me an opportunity to find a closer relative that might be a match."

Didar released his fist and spread his fingers open wide then shook his wrist and smoothed the bedsheet. *How do I respond to this? The last thing I need is Omar searching for relatives.* Didar cleared his throat. "There are no relatives, Omar. This is a waste of your time. And I've heard that insurance companies, like this GENmatch you talk about, deny people coverage for genetic reasons."

Omar moved closer to the bed and gazed down at him. "Dad, I realize we don't think there are any relatives, but what if there are?"

Didar searched Omar's face; a lump rose in his throat. Had he found out more than he let on?

"Doing this might save your life."

Didar tried to calm his breathing. His face burned and his ears rang. Worry burrowed in the creases of Omar's forehead.

"Listen Omar. Remember, this is my life and I don't want you putting your results on a public site where anyone can use them for any purpose. Let's just wait and see what the doctor says and how long the wait will be once I'm on the list."

"Okay Dad, rest. We can talk about this another time." Omar walked back to the chair in the corner of the room and sat down. "Just know, I've got your back. I'll be here to help you through this no matter how hard it is or how long it takes. Kidneys will not take you out. Understand?"

Didar smiled. Omar reminded him of himself, determined, confident and loyal, but so much better than his younger self. He didn't like to think about his life before Mahtob, before Omar. Because of them he'd turned his life around. He took a deep breath and exhaled. He owed his life to them.

"Okay Omar. You're right, I'm tired. And I consider this matter closed. No need to search for relatives that don't exist. We'll figure out another way."

As Omar settled into the chair, Didar closed his eyes but his transgressions circled his thoughts. He took deep breaths, his pulse still drumming in his ears.

The stress of Omar locating a relative overwhelmed him. What did he find through MyGeneticFamily? More than distant cousins? He hadn't been careful in his younger years and women seemed to throw themselves at him. Maybe he had children he knew nothing about. His sense of entitlement was stronger back then. His jaw ached from grinding his teeth. He needed to calm down. Getting all worked up wouldn't do him any good.

Didar turned to the window opening his eyes to search the sky outside. A gloomy day mirrored the turmoil in the pit of his stomach. Storm clouds brewed and lightning struck off in the distance. "Perhaps an omen of things to come," he muttered to himself as he rolled over and fell into a restless sleep.

CHAPTER SIX

"What flowers should we buy this week?" Omar let go of his dad's hand and ducked into the cooler. He stared into the pails of cut flowers on the floor and glanced up at the colours on the shelves above. They didn't look as beautiful from the underside, so he focused on the flowers he could look down on.

Red roses always caught his eye. He liked their fragrance. But he always picked roses when his dad let him choose. Today he'd pick something different. When he entered the cooler a wonderful, sweet, overpowering odour filled his lungs. Starting at one end of the cooler, he breathed in each pail, but none of them had the right smell.

"What's the matter, Omar? What're you looking for?"

Omar rubbed his nose. Everything smelled the same. "Can't you smell it, Dad? Something's sweet, but I can't figure out which flower it belongs to."

Didar closed his eyes and inhaled, then smiled. He reached above Omar's head and pulled down a pail of white flowers. Omar wrinkled his nose. White wasn't pretty. But he bent forward and took a deep breath. His eyes widened, and he stood back to study them. "They're not very colourful, are they?"

Didar smiled. "Seeing isn't the only way to experience beauty, Son."

Omar furrowed his brows before a smile spread across his face. "You mean the smell makes up for no colour?"

Didar patted Omar on the back. "Yes, well done. Sometimes we miss the magnificence of something because we think only our eyes discover beauty."

Omar felt a glow spread inside him, the one he always felt after praise. "What are these flowers called?"

"They're lilies. One of your mom's favourites."

"Really? Mom likes the flowers you buy every week so how do you know these are her favourite?"

"Because she picked them for her wedding bouquet."

Omar beamed. He knew which flowers to pick this week. He pulled five lilies out of the bucket and exited the cooler. The florist took them to the back saying she would add greenery to them. Omar didn't think they needed greenery, but he didn't want to question her. She always had a candy for him at the cash, so he suspected she knew what she was doing. They sat in chairs at the front of the store while she added the greenery.

"Dad, why do you buy flowers for Mom every week?"

A long pause ensued and Omar wondered if his dad heard him.

Finally, he responded.

"That's a fantastic question."

Omar grinned.

"Your mom is a special person. She saved my life."

Omar's eyes widened. "You almost died?"

Didar chuckled. "I didn't almost die, but I headed down a wrong path in life. Then I met your mom and I wanted to change my ways and be a good person so I could spend the rest of my life with her. And she forgave me for the things I'd done in the past."

Omar lowered his eyes. He couldn't imagine his dad not being a good person. But this was the second time he mentioned doing bad things. Omar didn't want to ask, but it weighed on him. "Like what Dad? What did you do that was so bad?"

Didar gazed out the window, and it took a long time for him to respond. "I hurt people, especially women. I didn't respect them like I should. Remember to always show respect to others, Omar. Everyone deserves respect."

Omar squinted up at his dad and creased his brow. "What's respect?"

"Oh, that's not an easy question to answer."

Omar sat patiently.

"Respect isn't one thing. It's different to every person."

Omar didn't see how that was helpful and opened his mouth to ask again when his dad continued.

"Because respect means something different to everyone, it's important to listen and figure out how they want to be treated. Learn about their priorities so you treat them right. Everything you say or do says something about your regard for them. Be kind, show concern and honour differences."

Omar tilted his head to one side. "Okay Dad, but what does respect have to do with flowers?"

Didar reached out and tussled Omar's hair. "Nothing. The flowers are a way to thank your mother for putting up with me. And to remind myself every week of her kindness and how she helped me be a better person. It's a small show of appreciation, but I want to be sure she knows I haven't forgotten how she gave me the benefit of the doubt so many years ago and trusted me to become a better person. I guess the flowers remind me to be respectful."

There were more questions Omar wanted to ask, but the florist returned from the back with flowers nestled in beautiful purple tissue paper, a white ribbon tied around the stems. Omar jumped to his feet.

"Here you go Omar. What do you think?"

"They're beautiful. My mom will like them." Omar glanced back at his dad who winked at him.

"Oh honey, your mom is one lucky lady."

"That's not what my dad says. He says he's lucky to have her."

Didar chuckled and glanced at the florist. Her face turned red, and she smiled in a way that told Omar he might have said something he shouldn't have. He stepped back holding the flowers, closed his eyes and breathed deeply.

"Omar, I have a little treat for you." The florist handed him a candy wrapped in purple metallic paper. The same colour as the tissue paper. Omar shifted the flowers to his left hand and reached for the candy, beaming.

"Thank you."

Back in the car Omar laid the flowers on the back seat and hopped in the front with his dad. "Next week could we buy some flowers for Lana? You know, to thank her for being so nice every week? She always has a candy for me."

Didar cleared his throat. "Sure Omar. I'm sure she'd like that."

CHAPTER SEVEN

"**I**s this Omar?" Jahana played with the corner of the tablecloth. She didn't want to make the call, but her curiosity got the best of her.

"Who's asking?"

An edge in his voice cut through the phone. Maybe she should hang up.

She paused. "Ah, it's Jahana, your sister." Silence filled the air. Her heart beat in her temples.

"Oh, Jahana." Omar cleared his throat and his voice softened. "So nice to hear from you."

"I hope you don't mind the call. I thought about messaging, but then decided I should just call. It would be a lot of back and forth typing."

Why hadn't she messaged? Talking to a brother she'd never met about a father she never wanted to meet was more than awkward.

"No, not at all. Like I said, nice to hear from you." Jahana heard Omar pull out a chair. She sighed. He had some time to sit and chat.

"I'm just calling to see if you have had any luck with GENmatch." Jahana massaged her neck with her free hand.

"No, I haven't posted my results yet. Dad doesn't want me to. And I'm hoping you change your mind and get tested. You're his best hope. It's unlikely more than distant cousins will show up. He only had one brother, and he died childless during the revolution."

Jahana clenched her jaw. "No, I haven't changed my mind. I'm not about to donate a kidney to a man who abandoned my mother." Jahana stopped short of bringing up her mother's sexual assault.

"You don't understand. My dad would never have left a pregnant woman. He would have been there for you."

Jahana bowed her head and realized she'd twisted the corner of the tablecloth until the hem unravelled. She clenched her fist around the frayed end and took a deep breath, restraining herself from blurting out the truth. "Have you told him about me?"

Another pause told her the answer before he replied. "No. I don't want to upset him right now. A spike in blood pressure could further damage his kidneys."

Jahana stood and paced the length of her kitchen. "Oh, we wouldn't want to upset him."

"What do you mean?" The naivety in Omar's voice couldn't be mistaken.

"Never mind." Jahana breathed deeply before continuing. It's clear you don't need my input. I'll let you go then." Jahana held the phone out to press the hang-up button when Omar's voice cut in.

"No, no. Thank you for the GENmatch suggestion. It's clear you have no intention of being tested or donating a kidney. I understand your position, I do. While I hoped to convince you otherwise, I'm not sure I'd do anything differently in your position. GENmatch is my only hope at this point. Thank you for suggesting it."

Jahana felt a twist in her stomach. If she wore his shoes, she'd be desperate to save her parent as well. "I'm sorry Omar. You must be so frantic. The mother who raised me recently died, and it's devastating to lose a parent. I'd have done anything for her. I hope GENmatch works out for you. Will you tell me if you get a match?"

Jahana stopped pacing and sat at the island. She pushed her hair back and clutched it between her fingers, her eyes closed. She wished she hadn't made this call.

"Sure, I'll let you know. I've always wanted a brother or sister. So sorry this is the way we have to connect."

Jahana's hand dropped and her head fell back leaving her staring at the ceiling. "I'm sorry too Omar. Until recently I didn't have any other siblings either and always wished I did. Good luck with everything."

"Thanks."

Jahana heard the disappointment in his voice. She wished she'd never connected with him. How could anything good come of this?

She laid the phone on the counter and poured herself a glass of iced tea; her throat suddenly dry. Was she being too judgmental? She might save a person's life and she refused. God wouldn't agree with her decision. But should she feel guilty about not giving a kidney to a man who raped her mother? Was she wrong to judge him and deny him what might be his life?

"Damn it." Jahana slammed her empty glass on the counter with more force than she intended and it cracked down one side.

"Mom are you okay?"

Jahana whirled around. "Oh yes, Sabah. I just set the glass down a little harder than expected. You startled me. I thought you were in your room reading?"

"I need some water."

Jahana reached into the cupboard for a glass and filled it. "Here you go. I think I'll go to bed and read as well. Do you want me to tuck you in?"

Sabah nodded and Jahana trailed her up the stairs to her bedroom. She needed to talk her decision over with someone. She'd like to talk to her baba, but this would upset him a lot. Maybe her cousin Mishal? Or maybe her biological mother? They hadn't communicated in a long time, although it was more her decision than her mother's. But perhaps her mother could help her justify why she refused to get tested. She needed to think it over before reaching out.

As Jahana turned off the light and crawled into bed, she thought about how there was something about Omar that sucked her in. As much as she didn't want to like him, she did. There was something familiar, yet she couldn't put her finger on it. Something in his voice that soothed her. She'd keep in touch with Omar and support him in ways she was able. It wasn't fair he had to deal with this. Losing a parent gutted you. And he loved his father. Could a rapist raise a son so different from himself? Could Didar be the good father Omar claimed him to be? Jahana shivered and pulled the covers up to her chin. She couldn't bear to think about the man her brother might really be.

****

"Hello Lana." The bell chimed as the door closed behind him.

"Why Omar, so nice to see you." Lana's face appeared drawn and her eyes sunken. "Your dad hasn't been in this week. Is everything okay?"

"Well, not exactly. He's still in the hospital. His kidneys didn't recover from an infection and he's on dialysis and needs a transplant. I'm not sure when he'll be well enough to come in. He asked me to drop by and get some flowers for Mom."

"So sorry to hear that." Lana's face turned ashen, and she fidgeted with a bouquet sitting on the counter.

"But I'm searching for a kidney donor and the doctor's say other than his kidneys he's in good health, and they think he'd do well on dialysis long term if need be. Are you okay Lana? I'm sorry, I didn't realize this news would upset you so much." Omar leaned forward and grasped her shoulder.

She turned away and waved him toward the cooler. "Oh, I'm fine, it's just a shock. He's always seemed so healthy." Omar noticed a quiver in her voice and her hand wipe her eyes as she strode to the back of the store.

"Just give me a shout when you've picked something out." Her voice cracked and trailed off.

Omar stepped into the cooler. The smell enveloped him in warm thoughts and good memories. Lana's reaction nagged at him. Didar chatted with her every week. Clearly, he'd made an impression. The effect he had on her said a lot about his dad's character. The aroma of the cooler brought him back to the task at hand. Red roses were the flower of the day it seemed. He picked out enough for two bouquets, one for Brie and one for his mom.

"Ready," Omar called out as he exited the cooler. Lana came from the back, more composed. "Could you make two bouquets please? One's for Brie."

"Keeping up your dad's tradition, are you?" Lana smiled and popped into the cooler before returning to the back to assemble the bouquets. He checked his phone. Brie would be at their house in an hour. She still stayed with Kathy and they hadn't talked further about the engagement, but he hoped maybe tonight they could make some headway. This was his last stop. The quiche, a baguette and a dessert pastry sat in packages on the front seat of the car. He'd throw a salad together when he got home.

Lana returned with three red rose bouquets. "I hope your dad gets out of the hospital soon. Tell him I'm thinking about him and praying he finds a kidney soon. Please give him this bouquet from me. And Omar, be sure to tell me if there's anything I can do." Lana strode around the counter and gave Omar a hug that lasted longer than he felt comfortable with.

"Oh, Lana, that's so kind of you. I'll pass on your best wishes." Omar backed away and turned to the door. He heard the bell on the inside of the door clang as it closed behind him. He wondered what his dad would think about getting red roses from the florist. It seemed kind of strange, but he was her best customer.

As Omar prepared dinner and set the table, he thought about the phone call from Jahana the evening before. Why was she being so selfish? He shouldn't expect it from her. But he usually convinced people to do what he wanted. Yet she refused to donate a kidney. Whether his dad wanted it, he needed to post his DNA results on GENmatch.

His phone dinged. Brie would be late.

With the table set, the quiche in the oven and salad ready for the dressing, Omar glanced at the clock. *No better time than the present.* With the preparatory work for GENmatch complete he just needed to post and pray for a match.

In the study he jarred the laptop to life. GENmatch opened and Omar faced the screen prompting him to post. His dad's words rang in his ear as he considered the implications. His DNA results would be public for anyone to use as they saw fit. Would this move come back to haunt him?

Don't be ridiculous. His finger hesitated over the enter key, then pressed down. The screen blinked, and a message indicated his results did not post. A quick scan revealed he hadn't checked the box confirming he'd read and understood their policies. Without scrolling through the pages of legalese, he clicked on the box and once again hit enter to publish.

The screen paused, and the cursor blinked, processing. Finally, results popped into view. A match notification stared back at him.

Don't get too excited. They're distant cousins. Heart beats thudded in his ear.

The mouse hovered, then he clicked on the results. The thunder of his heartbeat increased. A table of results stared back at him. The top match was strong. It took him a while to understand, but it appeared this person, a male, identified as having 50% of the same DNA. According to GENmatch, this meant he was a brother or a father.

"A father? That made no sense." There wasn't a chance in hell his dad posted his results. The upload of his results from MyGeneticFamily to GENmatch was direct; no room for transcription errors. He tried to contain his excitement. Had he just located a brother? And not a half-brother either, a full brother?

"Omar?" Brie's voice brought him back from his thoughts and he leaped to his feet.

"Sorry Brie, I didn't hear you come in." He embraced her, but she didn't return his earnestness and pulled away, holding him at arm- length.

"Are you all right Omar? What's up?"

How could she always read his mind? Tonight, was going to be about them, but he needed to talk to someone about what he found.

"Oh, there's so much I need to talk to you about. Come and I'll pour you a glass of wine."

Brie followed Omar into the kitchen. "Mmm something sure smells good."

"I'm just warming, not cooking. Hope you don't mind?"

Brie looked at him and raised her eyebrows. "Mind? Are you kidding? Less clean-up. More time to talk. It's all good."

Brie sat on the stool across the island and sipped her wine. Omar burst at the seams, but pulled himself together, drizzled dressing on the salad and removed the quiche from the oven. He plated the food and carried it to the dining room. The candles flickered, ready for the romantic dinner and conversation that would no longer occupy the evening. Brie followed carrying the glasses of wine, the bottle tucked under her arm.

Sitting across the table, Omar reached for her hand. Brie searched his eyes. "What is it?"

"I hoped to talk about us this evening, but just before you came, I received some news I need to run past you. My dad has preoccupied me the last few days…"

"Is your dad okay?" Brie's eyes widened, and she gripped Omar's hand.

"Yes, yes, it looks like he'll be going home soon. He'll have to go to the hospital three times a week for dialysis, but eventually they'll train him and Mom to do home dialysis. What I need to talk to you about is a DNA match I just learned about."

Brie reached for her wine with her free hand and took a sip. "Another match? Do you have another sibling?"

Omar picked up his fork and stabbed his quiche, it didn't separate like it should; a bit rubbery. He regretted putting it in the oven so early. "It looks that way. I can't be sure yet because the results could mean it's a full brother or a father. I share half of the same DNA with somebody else on GENmatch. Someone who identifies themselves as a male."

Omar watched Brie's reaction. She raised the slice of baguette to her mouth, but paused, her hand suspended in mid-air. She placed the bread back on her plate and stared at Omar.

"Has your dad had his DNA tested? Could it be him?"

"That's the thing Brie, my dad would never have his DNA tested, let alone post it to GENmatch. I told him about the MyGeneticFamily test a few days ago and about how I planned to post my results to GENmatch to hopefully find a match for him. He was livid and kind of over-reacted, saying insurance companies might use it against me and I shouldn't put that kind of information into the public domain."

Brie raised her hand between them. "Now wait a minute. Last I heard you were contacting your half-sister to see if she had the right blood type. What happened there?"

Omar chewed and swallowed his mouthful. "Unfortunately, she refuses to get tested even though her blood type matches. Understandably she's bitter about not knowing her father, but she suggested GENmatch. I hadn't even heard about it before."

Brie swirled her glass. "I've heard of it, but isn't it just another DNA testing site?"

Omar broke off a piece of baguette and took a bite. "MyGeneticFamily tests your DNA. GENmatch allows you to post your results so you can compare them with other people's results from other DNA testing venders. The site allows you to cast a larger net to find matches from people regardless of where they've had their DNA tested."

Brie stopped eating and listened. "And this is where your match came up? That's crazy."

Omar reached for his wine. "But if this is a brother, it would mean we share the same parents, both parents." Omar's eyebrows raised as he peered at Brie over his wine glass. She sat in silence, lips pursed, a frown on her face.

"It's okay Brie, say it. What're you thinking?"

Brie shifted in her chair. "I'm sure this is crossing your mind too, but it looks like you're adopted. Maybe your mom and dad aren't your biological parents? If that's the case this new match wouldn't be a match to donate a kidney either."

Omar pushed his plate away, no longer hungry. He took a large swallow of wine and cleared his throat. "It crossed my mind, but I hope that isn't the case. Maybe my parents put a child up for adoption?"

Brie patted Omar's hand. "That doesn't seem likely, but I suppose it's possible. What if the match isn't a brother, but a father that isn't Didar? Again, this wouldn't work out in your quest to find a kidney donor."

Omar lowered his head. "That's not good news either. Are there any possibilities other than my parents giving up a child for adoption that might work in my dad's favour as far as getting a kidney donor?"

Brie chuckled. "This is ridiculous. You look so much like your mother you have to be her child. But that might mean you and this potential brother have a dad other than the one who raised you. You can't be adopted."

Omar smiled. "True. So, if we rule out adoption what's…"

Brie interrupted, waving her hands in the air. "What about an identical twin? Could your dad have a sibling you know nothing about? I've heard that identical twins share the same DNA."

Omar shook his head. "Dad only had one sibling, and he died in the revolution in Iran. I'm sure he would have told me about an identical twin."

Brie sipped her wine, eyes sparkling. "Maybe he doesn't know about his twin. Maybe his parents gave up one of them when they were born. You hear about twins being separated at birth. Wouldn't it be great if you just found his identical twin? You couldn't ask for a better match for a kidney."

A smile spread across Omar's face. "That would be great" He sighed.

Brie set her glass down and leaned forward. "You need to reach out to this person and find out who they are."

"The twin thing's a possibility, perhaps more-so than the likelihood of adoption or my parents giving up a son or my dad posting his DNA to GENmatch."

Brie picked up her fork. "You just said your dad over-reacted when you brought up your DNA testing. Maybe he's afraid you'll find a twin or other relative he doesn't want you to know about?"

"Or maybe he's afraid I'll find a son he and my mother gave up for adoption? Or find out I'm adopted?" Omar could feel his dinner burning at the back of his throat.

"You could be right. But you'd think he'd be pleased to have a sibling, especially an identical twin. He'd definitely be a match for a kidney."

"It seems strange, but perhaps revealing a family secret isn't worth a kidney to him."

Omar reached for the bottle of wine and topped up their glasses. Maybe he could drink the whole mess away. An identical twin may save his father's life. But what if it turned out his dad wasn't his biological dad and no relative could donate a kidney? The only thing left to do was to reach out and find the face behind the DNA, but he'd talk to his dad first.

CHAPTER EIGHT

✄⊲⊳✄

"**W**hat do you mean, do I have a twin?" The veins on Didar's forehead throbbed in time to his heartbeat. The pressure rose in his temples. What the hell was Omar talking about?

"Now Dad, calm down. I didn't mean to upset you."

Didar closed his eyes, breathing in through his nose and out through his mouth. The nurse taught him this technique and told him to use it whenever he got worked up. But every time he breathed in; he smelled the roses Lana sent, and that didn't help. Red roses weren't a flower someone other than your wife sent you. She, above anyone, should have known that. When he opened his eyes, Omar sat in the chair at the end of the bed. Chin in his palms, staring at him.

"Okay. I'm calm. Now tell me what would possess you to ask if I had a twin?"

Omar raised his head but averted his eyes to the window as he replied. "I'm exploring all options. An identical twin would be the best match for a kidney, that's all. Any relatives you might have that I don't know about?"

Didar could always tell when his son skirted the truth. "Omar, you're aware of everything there is to know about my relatives. I only had the one brother. My parents have passed. I'm it. No other relatives. You may as well give up. No reason for you to post DNA results." Didar's voice trailed off as he realized why Omar asked these questions. "Omar, have you posted your results on that public website?"

Omar slapped his knees and stood. "Dad, it's the only hope we have of finding a match. If we wait for you to rise to the top of the transplant list, we'll be waiting at least five years, probably more. That's a lot of time."

"So, you have posted your results? Omar, why? I told you not to." Didar closed his eyes and slowed his breathing once again.

"Dad, we need to stop talking about this. It's upsetting you. I'm sorry I brought up the twin thing. Can we let it go?"

Didar's eyelids snapped open; Omar stared down at him. He recognized the imploring gaze. Even as a grown man, Omar still melted his heart with that look. Didar softened. Omar wanted to help. And he appreciated it. As much as he didn't want to admit it, fear rocked his soul. What if he didn't continue to do well on dialysis? He couldn't roll over and die. Sixty-nine was way too young. He promised Mahtob he'd slow down, and they'd travel. They couldn't do that now. But if he obtained a new kidney, maybe they could return to their dream.

"Okay, you're right. Probably best to let it go today. I don't want you doing something you'll regret. DNA on a public site is not something to take lightly."

Omar leaned over and patted Didar's shoulder. "I know Dad. I know."

Silence followed. Didar searched for something to talk about. He didn't want Omar to leave.

"So, how's Brie? Why doesn't she come with you to visit?"

A shadow crossed Omar's face.

"Is everything all right?"

Omar sat back down in the chair and again gazed out the window. "Oh sure, everything's fine. She's busy with work, but sends her love." Omar glanced at his father and smiled before shifting his focus to the sky again.

Didar searched for something else to talk about. Something safe that wouldn't upset either of them.

"How's the business? Everything running smoothly?" Didar realized this question had the potential to be a trigger. He had a hard time letting go of the business even though Omar ran things as well as he had.

Omar grinned and refocused his attention on Didar. "Yes, all is well. Profits are up and we're heading into the holiday season with lots of stock. The online sales have risen this year. There was a bit of a snag with deliveries last week, but we ironed out the problem and all is well. People are back to buying diamonds. The economy is picking up."

Didar beamed. "So proud of you, Son. It was the right move to step back and let a younger man take the helm. You've come in with fresh ideas. That's what the business needed."

Omar glanced down at his phone. "Oh Dad, sorry, I didn't realize what time it was. Speaking of business, I promised the Manhattan store I'd drop by today. Being Saturday, they're closing at six, so I better get going."

Didar hid his disappointment behind an expressionless mask. "No problem, Son. You head out. And say hi to Brie from me."

Omar rose, but before he reached the door, he stopped and turned. "Don't worry Dad, we'll figure something out and find that kidney soon."

Didar dismissed him with a wave of his hand. "No worries. Something will come up." Didar didn't believe his words. He watched Omar turn and pass through the doorway. The sound of his R.M. Williams boots faded as he strode down the hall and the elevator chimed.

Didar sat up in bed and swung his legs over the side facing the window. He choked back anger, sadness, and frustration, his fists landing on the bed beside him. There comes a day when the child becomes the parent. It shouldn't happen so soon.

****

"I'm at a loss. What should my next move be?"

Brie lounged on the couch. She dropped by for the third time this week. They hadn't talked about the engagement and she didn't sleep over, but things progressed. Omar tossed Brie a printed copy of the email he sent to the father match the previous week.

Upon posting my Ancestry.com results to GENmatch, it identified you as a close relative. Either a brother or a father. This confuses me because my father raised me and I don't have any siblings. I've come up with four possibilities to explain this match:

1. *The man who raised me posted his DNA results to GENmatch;*

2. *My mother had two children with another man;*

3. *I'm adopted; a brother is adopted; or*

4. *My father has an identical twin.*

None of these options seem plausible to me, so you can imagine my curiosity is piqued. I expect nothing from you. I only want to solve this mystery.

"This looks good Omar. There's nothing here that should upset anyone. I mean, any of those possibilities might be upsetting, but your tone in the email is good. Why don't you email him again?"

Omar sat on the couch and Brie stretched out from the other end. "I don't want to nag him and scare him away." Brie settled her feet in Omar's lap.

"I like that you didn't go into detail about why you posted your DNA. It's best you wait until you build some kind of relationship, but you need to reach out again."

Omar picked up Brie's feet and massaged them as he listened.

"You've waited a week. That wouldn't count as nagging. It might be very scary for them. What if they don't know they have a son? Or if it's your dad, he'll have to admit he posted his results. And if it's a twin, he might try to deal with a possibility he never imagined. You've given whoever it is enough time to get over their initial shock. Time to poke at them again."

Omar sighed. She confirmed what he had to do. He was eager to get answers, hoping for the identical twin option. How could his dad be unhappy to discover a sibling? Especially if that sibling donated a kidney. If his dad received the last email, he didn't act any different from normal, but Didar was good at keeping secrets. He'd kept things from his mom in the past. Nothing big; surprise parties and that sort of thing. But his acting skills were impressive. If the email went to him, Omar might never find out.

"You're right. Do you mind if I go do that right now?"

Brie pulled up her knees to let Omar move off the couch. "Of course not. Go ahead. I'll find a movie we both might like to watch."

Omar rose from the couch and bent down, dusting her forehead with a kiss. "I love you."

"I know you do." Brie stared back at him with tender eyes. He wanted nothing more than to lie down beside her, but he didn't want to push her. Instead he walked out of the room and into the study. He sat in front of the keyboard, contemplating where to begin.

> *I sent you an email last week, but have yet to receive a reply.*

Too judgmental. He highlighted the sentence and pressed delete. After an extended pause, he started again.

> *I understand my email last week may have been a shock to you. Let me reiterate, I'm not seeking anything from you. I want to solve the mystery of who's matching to me. If you're unsure of how we're related, let's figure it out together.*

Omar re-read his message, then hit send before over-thinking it. "Please respond," he muttered to himself. Guilt and fear turned his stomach. He hated the blatant lie. Of course, he sought something, a kidney; the reason for posting his results. What he might stir up brought acid up from his stomach. What if Didar wasn't his dad, and he didn't know? This might turn into a disaster.

Omar returned to the living room. Brie glanced up at him, apprehension pasted on her face. "What Brie?"

The corners of her mouth turned up a little. "Would it hit too close to home if we watched 'Philomena'?"

"What's it about?"

Brie rolled her eyes. "Sometimes I wonder if you ever listen to me?" But then she smiled. "We discussed this movie when it came out. It's about a mother who gave up her child and spent her lifetime searching for him. Too much? It's the only one I've found that we've both considered before."

Omar grinned, holding her feet up as he slid under them. "No, it's not too much. Maybe it'll give me some ideas about pursuing my identity."

Brie rolled onto her side and started the movie. Omar continued with the foot massage, pressing his thumbs into the arch of her foot. She smiled and sighed.

****

Jahana listened for one more ring before hanging up when a voice broke the ring pattern.

Jahana switched the phone to her left hand and cleared her throat before responding. "Hello Omar, this is Jahana."

"Oh, hello. Can you wait a minute?" He told someone he needed to take the call and footsteps echoed as he walked away.

"Sorry about that. I just finished up a meeting; so glad you called. I intended to call you later today."

The smile in his voice came through the phone. She hoped he didn't think she phoned to rescind her decision about kidney donation.

"I'm sorry to bother you at work, but I'm wondering if you posted your results to GENmatch?" It came out more abrupt than she hoped. She planned to start the conversation by asking about his dad's health, but truly she didn't care about him. She only worried about Omar. It seemed illogical she should care about someone she'd never met. If someone told her she would bond with a stranger that called himself a brother, she would have told them they were crazy.

"Yes, I posted my results, and found a match, but it's turned into a bit of a mystery."

Jahana's interest piqued. It didn't surprise her there would be other relatives. If Didar had assaulted her mother, she likely wasn't the only one. How many matches might Omar find? "What do you mean Omar? Is it a potential kidney donor?"

A long pause followed, and something rolled across the floor followed by a squeak. She imagined him settling into a plush office chair in a Manhattan corner office, tall windows overlooking the Hudson River.

"I'm unsure. You see Jahana, I matched to someone who carries 50% of my DNA. It's a father or a full brother. Neither of which makes any sense."

Jahana's jaw dropped, and she stammered, "Now, that's a surprise."

"I know, hey? I've gone over it in my head a million times. My, uh, girlfriend Brie and I have come up with some solutions but we're crossing our fingers it turns out to be an identical twin to my father, which would be a perfect kidney match. It might also mean I'm adopted or my mother had an affair and became pregnant from the same man twice. Not plausible options in my book. Of course, it might be my dad's DNA, but I can't imagine him getting tested, let alone posting his results on a public website."

Jahana swallowed. This might mean the man who raised Omar wasn't the rapist. She hoped for Omar's sake that was the case. Didar seemed to be a good father to Omar. Maybe, like her, Omar was adopted.

"Jahana, are you still there?"

"Ah, yes Omar, sorry. Just lost in my thoughts." She wanted to tell him her hopes, but she composed herself and reiterated his words. "So, either you're adopted and have a brother, your father has an identical twin, your mother had an affair and became pregnant twice, or your father posted his DNA. Those are quite the possibilities."

Jahana moved from sitting at the island in the kitchen to the couch in the living room. Her head spun.

"Yes, I'm sure I've considered all the possibilities. It's unlikely my dad posted his results because he's against making private information public. And I'm not sure I want to find out the story behind this mystery man, but the possibility he had an identical twin or I have a full brother gives me no choice. This might be the person who can donate a kidney. I've emailed, but so far no one's responded. It's very frustrating."

And stressful, Jahana thought. "Even though we barely know each other, I'm here for you. Please keep me in the loop. Oh, and I meant to ask, how is Didar?"

"Oh, he's okay. He hates being tied to the hospital with a strict dialysis schedule. But he's learning to cope. There's talk of dialysis training so he'll be able to do it at home eventually.

After more small talk Jahana ended the call and stretched out on the couch, running through all the possibilities. It was hard to imagine how difficult this must be for Omar. One thing she could do to ease his angst is get her blood typed to determine whether she was a match for Didar. A match, though, might suggest he's their father. It was a catch twenty-two. If she matched, she wouldn't want to donate a kidney and if she didn't match, she'd like to. Without thinking herself into paralysis, she googled how to get typed for a kidney transplant, and called to set up an appointment.

Catch twenty-two or not, she had to find out.

CHAPTER NINE

"**A**dopted, you're adopted!" Jimmy taunted Omar on the playground. No one got along with Jimmy and as far as Omar knew Jimmy didn't have any friends. He tried to walk away from him, but this time he felt the anger rise from his chest, up his neck until his ears burned.

"Am not!" Omar shifted from one foot to the other.

Jimmy was older and bigger than most kids and a bully. But Omar had had enough and stood his ground to face him toe to toe.

"Think about it bug eyes. You look nothing like your dad. I've seen him and I can assure you there's no family resemblance."

"Is too." Omar remained rooted to the spot, knees trembling.

"Ha-ha that's all you've got? Ever seen your birth certificate? I bet it shows father unknown. I take it back. You're not adopted, you're a bastard." Jimmy reached out and shoved Omar's shoulder, pushing him off balance.

Omar steadied himself and leaped at Jimmy, fists flying but not connecting with anything more than air. Then it happened; his fist hit something hard and Jimmy squealed. Omar withdrew and noted blood on his knuckles. He glanced from his hand to Jimmy, who lay on the ground groaning holding his bloodied nose. Omar's eyes widened. He'd just hit the big kid, the bully. Might as well quit school because he was as good as dead. Next chance Jimmy got he'd be the one on the ground and he'd be lucky if he could squeak out a groan.

Omar scanned the playground. A crowd gathered and the schoolyard monitor sprinted toward them. No sense running away. Enough kids saw what happened. He may as well stand and face it like a man. That's what his dad would want him to do.

"Back away, everybody, back away. Oh dear. Jimmy are you okay. Can you sit up?"

Jimmy glanced up at everyone staring at him. For once his voice was silenced and when he sat up, the blood gushed down his face. The monitor's eyes filled with panic. Her eyes rested on Omar.

"Omar, go into the school to the staff room and tell someone to bring ice. Off you go and be quick."

It was just the escape Omar needed. He raced toward the school, flew through the doors and ran down the hall. Normally someone would yell at him to slow down, but the halls were empty. He rounded the corner and ran straight into Mr. Phillips the principal.

"Whoa there, young man. What's the rush?"

"Jimmy's hurt. His face is bleeding and Mrs. Jenkins said to come get ice and some help." Omar panted and held his bloodied hand behind his back. He'd have to answer for what he'd done, but the longer he could put it off the better.

Mr. Phillips ducked into the staff room and came out carrying an ice pack. He didn't run, but hurried; it was doubtful his large frame and short legs could even run. Omar hung back and let him go.

"Looks like a nasty hand you've got there." Omar wheeled around. Mrs. Ranslam stood behind him. Her arms crossed and lips pursed. Omar stared at his feet. "Come with me." Her hand slid around the back of his head and pulled him forward into the staff room.

He'd never been in the staff room before. Couches and tables filled a sitting area, and a kitchen sat off to the side. Mrs. Ranslam led him to the sink where she turned on the water and reached for his hand. "Now this might hurt a little, but we need to get the blood and dirt off to see what kind of damage we're looking at.

Omar squeezed back the tears. He refused to cry. For the first time in his life he'd won a fight. Winners don't cry.

As the blood and dirt washed away, swollen knuckles of a purple hue remained. There'd be no hiding this from his mom and dad. Would he get suspended from school?

"Okay, after I wrap your hand up in paper towels, I'll leave you sitting beside Mr. Mankle while I go call your parents. You need to get an x-ray to be sure nothing's broken."

Omar sat quietly. Mr. Mankle wasn't the talkative type and just left him to his thoughts. Soon he heard his mother's voice drifting down the hall. Why hadn't they called his dad? He'd better understand why he stood up for himself.

"Omar! What've you done?"

Mrs. Ranslam ran interference. "Now, we haven't sorted this out yet and I think that can wait till tomorrow. It appears Jimmy and Omar had an altercation, but the important thing right now is for a doctor to examine that hand. I'm sure you understand Mrs. Fassid."

Omar envisioned his mom dragging him down the hall by his ear, but she put her arm around him and led him to the car. Once in the car, the silence shattered. "Omar, what were you thinking? What did you do? And why? Since when do you go around hitting people?"

Omar stared at his hand no longer wrapped in paper towels. The purple deepened by the minute. And it throbbed. "Jimmy said I'm adopted or a..." His words trailed away. He couldn't repeat that word to his mom. The car pulled away from the curb

"Or a what?" Mahtob glanced at her son then returned her gaze to the road.

"Uh, he said I'm adopted. He wouldn't stop taunting me." Omar dared to glance at his mom. Her face remained red, but the anger in her eyes lessened.

"Adopted. Oh Omar, kids go through a phase where they think everyone is adopted. Why on God's green earth would that prompt you to hit him?"

Omar sucked in air struggling to keep the tears at bay. "He told me I looked nothing like Dad so I must be adopted. And then he called me a bad word." It was no use. The tears overflowed and Omar made the ugly sucking noises that come with the release of tears held back too long. He turned his head to stare out the side window, praying he wouldn't see anyone he knew.

"Oh Omar. Jimmy tried to get a rise out of you and by the looks of it he did." Mahtob reached over and stroked his head. Omar peeked over at her. Her skin returned to its normal colour; her hard edges now soft. Omar ran a sleeve across his nose and smeared his tears with the back of his good hand. His fighting hand throbbed. Tears subsided and he let out a staccato sigh as he resigned himself to whatever fate would deal him.

"Omar, you don't look like your dad." Omar turned to his mom, mouth agape. "But that's because you take after me. I guarantee we did not adopt you. And you do have many of your dad's traits."

Omar sat in silence pondering his mother's words. He had no reason not to believe her. Besides, his dad was his hero. Didar had to be his dad.

CHAPTER TEN

"**I** told you not to post your results to GENmatch. What's the matter with you, boy!" Didar's face burned and sweat trickled down his forehead.

"Dad, we've been through this. I'm 34 years old for Christ's sake. I'll post my DNA if I bloody well want to." The vein above Omar's right temple pulsed.

Didar expected his did too. He took two deep breaths and closed his eyes. He wasn't supposed to get upset.

"Dad I'm doing this for you."

Didar's eyes sprang open. "I don't want you to do this for me! That's the point. If you're doing it for me, then I should have the right to say don't." Didar suddenly felt weak. He stumbled across the room and dropped into a chair.

"Dad are you okay?"

The concern in his son's eyes caused Didar to shudder. It was hard enough to deal with the reality of failing kidneys, but to see how it affected Omar broke his heart.

"No." Didar hung his head and took long breaths. "I need to go to the hospital." Didar hated how his blood pressure spiked. Usually he could settle it, but this time it felt different.

"Oh Dad, I'm so sorry. I didn't mean to upset you." Omar kneeled down in front of him.

Didar motioned for Omar to help him up. The room spun. Together they left through the front door and Omar helped him into the Cayenne's passenger seat.

****

"As you suspected, your blood pressure's out of control. We'll keep you for a day or two until you're stabilized." Didar stared at the ceiling. Tears stung the corners of his eyes. He turned his head. Omar sat to the side of the bed; head bowed. When the nurse left the room, Didar wiped his eyes and motioned for Omar to come closer.

"Now listen to me. This is not your fault. I asked you a question, and you answered me. Didn't I bring you up to be honest?" Didar feigned a smile.

Omar didn't return it.

"I won't ask you any more questions about your DNA post. I'll trust if you find someone to donate a kidney, you'll come to me."

Omar nodded, but Didar worried whether his son would tell him anything about his search for a kidney again. Maybe that was best. Didar would focus on the five-year transplant list plan and Omar would do whatever he wanted, anyway. His DNA results were public. There was no taking it back. They were out there for the world to see. *Maybe I'm better off dead. Do I want to know what those DNA results reveal?* Worry rooted in the back of his mind, an annoying niggle that swelled in intensity. He needed to focus on getting out of the hospital and back home.

****

"Oh my God, Brie. A message just popped up on my phone from the person who matched with me. They've finally responded."

Omar touched the GENmatch message, and it opened.

"Read it out loud. Don't keep me in suspense." Brie steered the car onto Beekman Street.

"Oh sorry. It's not very long.

Dear Omar,

Sorry I didn't respond sooner. I'd like to arrange a face-to-face meeting with you. Where do you live? I'll come to your city. We can meet somewhere public. Let me know where and when and I'll be there.

"That's it? He seems mysterious." Brie glanced at Omar before returning her attention to the road.

"Why wouldn't he want to share information by email before meeting? How should I respond?" Omar's stomach turned. Something wasn't right about this.

"You don't have a choice, do you? Why don't you set up a meeting for Saturday? That gives him a few days to get here. I can come along if you like?"

Omar glanced up. She was the best thing that ever happened to him. "Thank you. I'd like you to be there. Abraco's on east eighty-first and seventh street?"

"Sure, it's small enough we'd find him, but large enough to have some privacy. They get busy on Saturday's though. We'd have to make it later in the day when things get quieter."

Brie pulled in front of the restaurant. The valet waved and made his way toward them. Omar released the seatbelt and opened his door still focused on his phone and typing his response.

"Does he have a name?" Brie slipped her hand inside Omar's elbow.

"Ah, no. He didn't give me a name and his alias on GENmatch is a number." Omar finished typing and slid

74

his hand inside Brie's. "Do you mind if I read what I've typed back to him before I hit send?"

"Of course not."

The hostess greeted them as they entered the restaurant and seated them at their usual table.

"Okay, so here's what I've written so far." Omar sat forward and Brie leaned in.

> *Thank you for responding to my email. I'm excited to figure out how we're related. It's very kind of you to offer to meet in my city. I live in New York. If this Saturday works, we can meet at Abraco in Manhattan. Say 4 pm? Or if you prefer, we could communicate over email. Where are you coming from? And what's your name? My girlfriend will be with me. Hope to hear from you soon.*

Omar set his phone down on the table and searched Brie's face for guidance. Just as she opened her mouth to respond, the server showed up requesting drink orders.

"I'll have a Manhattan," Omar winked at Brie.

She laughed and responded, "And I'll have the same."

"Is it okay?" Omar asked Brie when the waitress moved on to the next table.

"It's fine. Do you want to ask him how old he is? That might give you an idea of how he's related?"

"I considered that, but decided it might be too pushy. He wants to discuss our relationship in person and I don't want to scare him off. It took long enough for him to respond. Is it too desperate if I reply right away or should I wait till tomorrow?" Omar rubbed his neck. A stress headache settled into the base of his skull.

"Definitely respond right away. This guy might have to travel a long distance. He'll need time to plan his trip. It's already Tuesday evening. Not everyone lives on their phone like we do. Best to catch him while he might still pay attention."

"Okay, here goes." Omar pressed send, placing the phone on the table face down. "Enough distractions, let's have a nice relaxing evening together. What are you ordering? Should we get something to share to start? The charcuterie?"

"Sounds perfect." Brie closed her menu, a contented smile lighting her face. "Omar, I feel like you're really working on your anger management and I want you to know I appreciate it. I feel like we're getting along better. Do you feel it too?"

"I've felt it too, and I really am trying. I sure miss you. Not that I'm trying to put pressure on you or anything. But whenever you're ready to move back in, I'm ready too." Brie bowed her head and Omar sensed he'd pushed too far.

"I know you're ready Omar. But I need more time. I like how things are right now."

Omar sighed. He hoped she'd feel comfortable with him and be ready to move back in. He'd just have to be more patient.

The table vibrated as Omar's phone buzzed. He flipped it over and glanced at the notification; a response.

"Sorry Brie, he's responded. Do you mind?" Omar opened the message before she replied.

"Of course not. As long as you read it out loud to me too."

The screen jumped to life revealing a short response.

Omar cleared his throat. "Abraco in Manhattan at 4:00 pm works for me. My name is John. I'll message you when I arrive and tell you what I'm wearing so you can pick me out of the crowd. See you then."

"I'm not liking this Brie. Something's off. He didn't tell me where he's coming from either." Brie sat forward and placed her hand over his.

"Let's just suspend judgement and see how this plays out."

She was right. There was no sense jumping to conclusions. It would all become clear in a few days.

****

Omar and Brie battled the freak snowstorm and entered Abraco's just before four. The weather kept people away so it was quiet. Omar kept checking his phone, but so far, no message from John. They walked up to the counter and ordered espressos. He'd never seen it so quiet.

A gust of cold air blew in through the open door. Omar and Brie turned to watch a woman and her daughter walk in. Omar raised an eyebrow at Brie. They didn't exchange words.

With espressos in hand they settled on a table away from the door. Brie sat with her back to the door, Omar faced it expectantly. It opened again, this time an older gentleman stumbled in. He stopped, stomped his feet and proceeded to the counter. His eyes glued to the menu board, not looking for anyone he might be meeting.

"Perhaps he's delayed because of the weather," Brie offered. She tried to give him hope, but hope seemed elusive. What if the mystery man decided he didn't want to show up? The door opened again. A middle-aged man stopped, scanned the tables rested his gaze on Omar and Brie. Omar glanced around and realized they were the only couple in the coffee shop. The man smiled at him and sauntered toward the table.

Tall and fit. A trimmed moustache graced his upper lip, his light hair short and cropped close to the scalp. Crow's feet and slight greying at the temples put him in his 40's. By appearance, Omar would never guess him to be a relative.

"Here he comes," Omar murmured to Brie. Brie turned her head just as the stranger reached the table. Omar stood and offered his hand.

"I'm Omar, you must be John." The man struggled to remove his glove, then grasped Omar's hand. Despite the cold weather, his hand was warm. Sweaty in fact.

"Pleased to meet you." John smiled a bit too forcefully.

"Oh, and this is my, uh, my girlfriend, Brie." Omar blushed. He still wanted to call her his fiancé. Brie rose, smiled and also shook hands.

"Please have a seat." Omar gestured to the chair next to him.

"If you don't mind, I'll grab a coffee first." John headed to the counter after placing his gloves on the table. Brie and Omar sat down.

"Awkward," Brie whispered. "But he seems nice enough. Doesn't look like you though."

"I'll say. How can he be a brother or father? It's obvious he's not an identical twin.

"Damn. So much for a perfect kidney match." Omar and Brie sat in silence waiting for John to return.

"Thanks for waiting, crazy weather out there." John slid into the chair beside Omar, set down his coffee and removed his jacket.

"Certainly is. Could be a long winter if it's starting this early. So, John, where is it you come from?" Brie leaned in.

"Oh, I live here in New York. Good thing. Not sure I'd have made it if I had to fly in. Flights were delayed all night because of the storm." John took a tentative sip of his coffee and let out a satisfied sigh. "Good choice." He waved his hand in reference to the coffee shop.

"One of our favourites. I worried it would be too busy, but the weather has kept the masses away. Guess that's something to be thankful for." Omar fidgeted. Time to get down to the meat of the conversation.

"Before we get started, please understand I'm not the man behind the DNA. I mean I posted the DNA, but it's not mine. I'm searching for a match for a client."

Omar relaxed. That explained a lot. Identical twin returned to the list of possibilities. He heard of people hiring others to find relatives.

"So how well do you know your client?" Omar tried to quiet his bouncing knee.

"Fairly well. Do you have any guesses as to how you might be related?" John took another sip of coffee.

Omar frowned, he hoped John had some answers. "Well since we share 50% of the same DNA, that means he's a brother, a father or an identical twin to my father. Would you say that's a fair assessment?"

John cracked open a new Moleskine notepad. He reached into his shirt pocket and retrieved a pen.

"Do you mind?" John held up the notepad and pen. "I want to make sure I capture everything." Omar glanced at Brie across the table. Their eyes met. Prickles tickled the back of Omar's neck. They both knew the other's thoughts. This was definitely strange.

"I guess not. But I can't imagine anything I have to say worthy of jotting down."

"How about we start with the people you know you're related to? Do you have siblings? Are your parents alive?"

"Sure, I guess we could start there. I'm an only child...as far as I'm aware." Omar paused and licked his lips. "My parents are alive. My dad had a brother, but he died years ago."

"So, tell me about your dad."

"Um, well, his name is Didar Fassid. Let's see, he was born in Tehran and immigrated to the U.S. in 1979. He came straight to New York, married my mom a couple years later and built up a chain of jewellery stores. You may have heard of them, Fassid Jewellers?" Omar stopped. What kind of information did this guy want? The conversation seemed one sided so far.

"Oh yes, I'm familiar with that chain. My sister shops there." John stopped writing and reached for his coffee.

"So, John, what can you tell us about your client?" Omar watched John place his coffee on the table before picking up his pen and click the end a few times. Perhaps a nervous habit?

"Well, I can tell you he lived in New York in 1980. He's Persian and in his mid to late sixties."

Omar grinned. "That sounds just like my father."

John cleared his throat, laid his pen on the table, and stared at Omar. "There's no easy way to say this Omar, a DNA sample from a rape and murder cold case led me to you."

CHAPTER ELEVEN

Omar and Brie glanced at each other.
Neither saw this coming. A guttural laugh
emerged from Omar.

"Is this some kind of sick joke? Who are you?" Omar
pushed his chair back ready to get up and leave. But the
look on Brie's face stopped him and he slid his chair
forward and met John's gaze. John was serious. Omar's fist
hit the table and John's coffee spilled over the side of his
cup, pooling on the low spot of the table. "This is
ridiculous!" Omar boomed.

John shifted in his seat, perched forward on his chair, and rested both hands on the table. "I know it's a shock. I need to speak with your father."

Brie reached across the table to calm Omar, but he pulled his hand away. She kicked his shin under the table and he whipped his head toward her. One look and he realized he needed to calm down.

He cleared his throat. "Who are you?"

John reached into his pocket and pulled out what at first appeared to be a small billfold. When he opened it up and laid it on the table, an audible groan emerged from somewhere deep within Omar.

"My name is John Brown. I'm a detective with the New York City police. Your DNA results matched a suspect's DNA we posted on GENmatch. We needed to meet with you to confirm suspicions that our cold case DNA likely belongs to your father. We'll need a sample from your father to confirm this."

Omar glanced at Brie. She sat still; eyes wide, complexion suddenly ashen. Omar recalled a news story awhile back about a serial murderer being apprehended through DNA testing. He hadn't thought about it again. There was no reason to, until now.

Omar cleared his throat and quietly asked, "What are the details of the cold case?"

John leaned back in his chair his fingers toying with his well-groomed moustache. "The case is of a rape and murder that took place in June 1980. The DNA came from a semen sample obtained off the victim and skin found under her fingernails." Omar felt the blood drain from his face. Silence ensued.

"We'll need to speak to your father." John's voice barely a whisper, almost apologetic.

Omar shook his head. "That's impossible. He's in the hospital in kidney failure. He's not supposed to get upset. A spike in blood pressure could kill him."

John again shifted in his chair. "A sample is needed to confirm the match. We could go in undercover, get a DNA sample and be out before he knew we were there. A hair, a cup he drank from. That's all it takes. We wouldn't have to upset him if it turns out he's not the person we think he is."

Omar shook his head. "I don't want you going anywhere near my dad. I'll get you a sample."

A long pause followed as John considered this possibility. "I don't mean to sound unsympathetic, but we don't need your permission."

Omar opened his mouth to object, but John raised his hand and continued. "However, we could accommodate your request. Whether or not your sample matches, we'll need another sample collected through the proper chain of command protocol. Since this is a sensitive situation, we can allow you to collect the sample first. I realize you may not believe it could be your father's DNA we have on file, but unless he isn't your biological father, I can assure you the DNA will be a match."

Omar nodded. What choice did he have?

John leaned forward. "You'll need to use gloves when collecting the sample to ensure you don't contaminate it with your DNA. Put the sample in a Ziploc bag and contact me. I'll come pick it up. You have 24 hours. If I don't hear from you by tomorrow afternoon at five, we'll be showing up at your dad's bedside."

Again, Omar nodded.

****

The rubber gloves and Ziploc felt like a rock in his jacket pocket. Omar massaged them between his fingers.

"Sorry I couldn't stay longer, Dad. Brie's meeting me for lunch and I need to get back to the office this afternoon. Are you sure you don't need anything?"

Didar was a chameleon; his skin turning as pale as the over washed sheets. "No, Son, I'm fine. I just want to get home. I'm so tired of this bed and this room. You give that girlfriend of yours a hug from me."

"Will do Dad. I'm just going to use your bathroom before I head out." Omar held his breath as he pulled the door closed behind him. He flicked on the fan, hoping to mask any noises he might make while searching for something to give him a good DNA sample.

He raised the lid on the toilet and unzipped his pants while scanning the room. His dad's toothbrush perched on the shelf above the sink. It would be perfect, but would also be missed. Beads of perspiration formed on his forehead. The temperature in the hospital was warm, but his sweating had nothing to do with the ambient temperature. He flushed and zipped, checking the back of the toilet for stray hairs. Nothing. He turned on the tap and noticed a hair flush down the drain. Damn. He should have checked the sink before turning on the water. His dad's hair brush sat on the shelf beside the toothpaste. He dried his hands and struggled into the rubber gloves. He fumbled with the Ziploc, opening it, then inserting the hair brush. Pay dirt. Hair unwound itself from the brush as he massaged the bristles. Some hairs had roots still attached which, according to John was important. After removing the brush, he held the bag up to the light. It appeared there were a few hairs that had a small bulge at their base. He sealed the bag and returned the brush to the shelf. Damn, he hadn't made mental notes about the direction it faced. Hopefully his dad didn't always put it down the same way. He stuffed the bag and gloves in his pocket, glanced at himself in the mirror and wiped the sweat from his forehead. As he lowered his right hand, he bumped the brush, and it fell into the sink.

"What's going on in there?"

"Sorry Dad, I just bumped your hair brush, and it fell into the sink." He breathed a deep sigh. Now he didn't have to worry about his dad realizing he'd moved the brush. He stared at his reflection. His dad didn't deserve to be lied to.

"Sorry about that Dad." Omar forced a grin as he emerged from the bathroom.

Didar waved his hand at him. "No worries. Now go meet that beautiful girlfriend of yours."

Omar stepped into the hallway and headed for the elevator. He pulled out his phone and dialled the number John gave him the day before.

"Just left Dad's hospital room. I've got some hair from his brush. Where do you want to meet?"

"That's great, how about I come to you? I can be at the hospital in half an hour. Meet you in the cafeteria?"

Omar didn't want to hang around, but it was as good a place as any and besides he could use a coffee.

As he settled into a seat by the window, he heard someone call out his name and turned. Lana from the flower shop made her way from the checkout to him.

"Lana, this is a surprise. What brings you here?"

"Oh, I just thought I'd stop by and see your father. I hope you don't mind. I felt so terrible after you left the store the other day and thought I'd stop in for a short visit. Is he able to have coffee?" She glanced at her hands, a coffee in each.

Omar thought it odd she would come by, but then there had been a steady stream of business associates dropping in too, and his dad liked the company. "Sure, I think it's fine. Just check with the nursing station first. Do you know where his room is?"

"Yes, I stopped at the information desk on the way in. Well, I better get up there before these coffees get too cold. Are you heading up too?"

Omar realized his dad would hear he didn't leave to meet Brie as he had told him. "Ah, no. I just came from there. I'm on my way to meet my girlfriend, but needed a coffee and had to make a couple calls so thought I'd sit a minute and take care of things rather than try to juggle it all while driving." He'd never been a good liar.

"Well, okay then. Talk to you another time."

Just as she turned to leave, John entered the cafeteria and scanned the room. He raised his hand and John made his way over and sat down opposite him.

Without a word, Omar took the baggie out of his pocket and slid it across the table. He noted Lana exit the cafeteria. John glanced at the bag and put it in his briefcase.

"I'm sure that wasn't easy for you to do, Omar. Thank you. I'll get this off to the lab."

Omar shifted in his seat. He swallowed hard and forced a smile. "Well, the sample will come back negative and you can move on to finding the real suspect."

John lowered his gaze and scratched at something crusted on the table. "Regardless of the results we must collect a new sample and follow a process to ensure the sample tested is from your father."

"Yeah, I remember. At least I'll be able to tell my dad you're barking up the wrong tree by that point. How long will it take to get a result?"

"Usually takes 72 hours, but I'm putting a rush on this, so we may get results sooner. Now I'll ask you to keep this between you and your girlfriend. I don't want you telling anyone else. Understand?"

"Ah yeah, I understand. Trust me, I won't be letting anyone in on this. It's not something I want to explain to anyone." Omar pushed his chair back and rose, then paused before walking away. "Will you give me the courtesy of telling me the results before you approach my father for another sample?"

John rose from his chair and reached out to shake Omar's hand, but Omar kept his hands buried in his pockets. John let his hand fall to his side. "Yes, I can do that. I'll call you as soon as I get the results from the lab."

Omar turned abruptly and shuffled out of the cafeteria. As he entered the main entrance, Mahtob headed straight to the elevator without noticing him. Omar wondered if his mom had ever met Lana. He pushed open the door and headed to the parking lot.

CHAPTER TWELVE

‟**O**mar, I've tried to be patient; have you figured out who the mystery man is yet?"

A squeak that sounded like Omar shifting in his office chair filled the silence on the other end of the phone. An extended pause ended when he cleared his throat. "That's a loaded question. It's a bit complicated."

Jahana chuckled. "Well, I'm not surprised. The last we talked it was complicated. Is it a father or a brother or an identical twin to your father?" Another long pause followed before Omar answered.

"I'm not supposed to talk about this, sorry."

"Really Omar? What the heck?" Jahana tried to make light of it, but her stomach turned.

"I'm sorry Jahana, but I've been sworn to secrecy."

"Okay, Omar, that's ridiculous. Who am I going to tell? And what could possibly be so secret?" Jahana swallowed. All kinds of things popped into her head that he might not want to talk about.

Omar sat silent before relenting. "Okay, but you have to promise you won't say anything to anyone."

"I promise. Tell me, what is it?" Jahana closed her office door and settled into her chair.

"The match contacted me, and my girlfriend Brie and I met with him. Turns out he wasn't the match, but rather a police officer who thinks their cold-case suspect is our dad."

It was Jahana's turn to create a dead-space in their conversation. The blood drained from her extremities and pooled in her torso. She dreaded the answer, but had to ask. "What are the details of the cold case?"

Omar explained the case, but his voice seemed to echo down a long pipe. 'Murderer' and 'rapist' reverberated in her head. Anger seethed in Omar's voice as he explained how Didar couldn't be the man they looked for. But that would mean he wasn't Omar's biological father. The best of the two possibilities would have seemed the worst possibility not that long ago.

Jahana swallowed. "Um, Omar, before you go on, there's something I have to tell you." When Omar didn't respond, Jahana asked, "Are you listening?"

"Yes, but something tells me I'll wish I wasn't."

Jahana decided it best to just say it. Tear off the band aid, so to speak. "The reason I haven't wanted to donate a kidney has nothing to do with me being angry at him for abandoning me and my mother, but rather to do with how my mother became pregnant. My mom, a Jew living in Tehran, was seventeen when she was raped. Your dad followed her home one day, pulled her into an alley, and attacked her. I'm a product of that rape."

Jahana heard deep breaths over the phone. "Omar, say something." She waited for his response.

"Seems strange you waited to tell me this till now. Why didn't you tell me before?"

"Would you have listened? Would you have talked to me again?"

"You're the only hope my dad has of getting a kidney. No, that came out wrong. You're also my sister. You don't know our dad. If you did, you wouldn't believe it either."

Jahana rubbed her temples. Maybe the monster who donated his DNA to them was still a stranger to them both.

"When will they tell you the results?"

"Well, it's been two days since I handed over the sample. They said it might take three, but expected it would happen quicker than that. So anytime now. I'm a wreck, but there's no way my dad did what you or the police say he's done."

"I hope Didar isn't our biological father. This must be so hard on you. Will you let me know when the police contact you?"

"Yeah. In the meantime, will you get tested to see if you're a match for a transplant?"

Jahana took a deep breath. How could she say no at this point? He needed something to hold on to. "Okay, I will. But it doesn't mean I'll donate if I'm a match, just that I'll get the testing started."

Jahana sat in her office, numbed by the news. If she matched for a kidney donation, it would likely mean Didar was their father and she'd have to tell Omar she wouldn't donate. If she didn't match, Omar would have to look elsewhere. It was truly a no-win situation. Yet her conscience tugged at her. Could she really withhold a kidney from another human being? Could she be that cold-hearted? She knew she couldn't. And maybe, like Omar, she wouldn't be a match. She turned to her computer and googled who to contact for tissue typing.

****

Omar walked into the room and Didar sensed something was wrong. His face ashen, eyes sunken and stare lifeless. He averted his gaze, refusing to look him in the eye. Omar stood at the foot of the bed and leaned on the footboard. White knuckles betraying his angst.

"What is it, Son?" Didar sat up in bed. He reached for Omar's hand, but Omar held back. "What's wrong?"

Omar's eyes lifted and tears pooled. He let go of the footboard and wiped his nose letting out a strangled cough before speaking. "Dad…" He paused, smacking the footboard as he turned to stare out the window.

"Just say it Omar. Whatever you have to say, I'll listen. Is it your mother? Has something happened?" Didar's heart raced. He swung his knees over the side of the bed, pushing his body up with his hands. Omar turned back and raised his hand for him to stop.

"No Dad, Mom's fine. Please stay in bed."

Didar remained sitting with his legs over the side, not sure whether to ignore his son. "Listen Omar, I can't imagine that what you have to say is worse than the things I'm conjuring in my head. If you're worried about raising my blood pressure, it's already up there. Now, just tell me. What is it?"

The mention of his blood pressure seemed to resolve something for Omar. He leaned against the windowsill and motioned for Didar to lay back in bed. "Okay, okay, I'll tell you. But promise me you'll try to remain calm."

Didar raised his legs and pulled the sheet up. "It's the business isn't it? What's going on?"

"No Dad, it's not the business. Just let me talk without interrupting until I'm done okay?"

"Okay, Son. I'm listening." Didar took a deep breath and tried to calm himself. *Breathe in through the nose, out through the mouth.*

"So, Dad, you remember when I posted my DNA results to GENmatch to find you a kidney?"

Didar nodded, being careful not to interrupt and reiterate how stupid his actions were.

"Well, I found a match right away. Someone with 50% shared DNA."

Didar scanned Omar's face, searching for a clue that would tell him what these results meant. It didn't appear to be good news. Fifty percent sounded good to him, but clearly not enough to be a donor or Omar would be ecstatic.

"I reached out to the person, and it took them awhile to respond, but eventually they did and we met at Abraco's."

So far this all sounded positive. The person must not have wanted to donate a kidney. That must be why Omar was so upset.

Omar took a breath and continued. "I need to back track a bit, Dad. Fifty percent shared DNA means the person is a brother, a father or an identical twin to a father. You would never have your DNA tested, let alone posted to a public website, so I assumed this person would be a brother or better yet, your twin."

Didar raised his hand. "You don't want me to interrupt, but this is nonsense. You're my only son and my only brother died years ago. This makes no sense Omar."

"It made no sense to me either. But it will if you let me finish."

Didar took another deep breath. Omar made more of this than need be. This guy had to be a quack and Omar was disappointed he didn't turn out to be a viable donor.

"Brie went with me to Abraco's. And it's a good thing she did because what this guy said had me so upset, I almost walked out on him." Didar drummed his fingers on the bed, but held his tongue waiting for Omar to get the story out.

"This guy said he represented the person whose DNA was the match. At the time it made sense. Lots of people hire professionals to investigate genealogy, so I figured this guy was legit. After asking me questions about my father, he told me the DNA posted to GENmatch, was likely yours."

Didar had enough. "Omar, this guy's scamming you. I don't know what reason he has to carry on like this, but I can one hundred percent tell you I have never had my DNA tested, let alone posted it to a website."

Omar raised his hand again. "You didn't post it, Dad, but someone else did."

Didar felt his pulse quicken and the ringing, rise in his ears. Who would post his DNA? His mind raced. He could see Omar doing it, to find a kidney donor, but clearly that wasn't the case. Didar closed his eyes and concentrated on his breathing.

"Are you okay Dad?"

Didar raised his hand. "Just give me a minute."

He opened his eyes and tried to read his son's thoughts, but Omar turned to the window. He told him not to post his results. Nothing good would come out of this.

"Okay, Son, continue. Who had my DNA tested and posted my results?"

Omar turned back to face him. He paused searching for the right words, but blurted out what he'd been holding in. "Police, Dad. The police tested your DNA and posted the results."

Ringing shrieked in Didar's ears. Omar's mouth continued to move. He raised his hands to his ears to shut out the noise, but the ringing came from within. He closed his eyes and counted. The ringing subsided. When he looked up, Omar stared at him, tears sliding down his cheeks. He lowered his hands.

"I wasn't shutting you out, Son, just trying to lower my blood pressure. Please tell me why the police had my DNA." Didar knew someday his past would come back to haunt him. He tried to lead a good life after he met Mahtob and he worked at atoning for his sins. He knew what Omar might tell him, but he needed to hear him say it.

"The DNA was from a cold case that involved a rape." There was a significant pause before Omar added, "and a murder."

Didar's face burned. The ringing in his ears surged again. "That's ridiculous. There's been a mix up."

"That's what I thought too Dad. They wanted to talk to you and collect a sample to confirm their DNA testing, but I was so sure they'd made a mistake, I convinced them to let me get a sample, so as not to upset you."

"You what?" Didar's voice boomed and echoed in his ears, the ringing obliterating any sounds Omar might try to speak. Didar counted again. This time out loud. Omar stood back; eyes full of anguish. After a few minutes, Didar in a more controlled voice, repeated, "What did you do, Omar?"

"I took some of your hair from your brush and gave it to the police. They tested it and it came back a perfect match. I wanted to tell you myself. They're waiting in the hall and will be in to recollect samples."

Omar dropped to the floor, kneeling at the side of the bed, choking back tears. He reached across and grasped Didar's hand. "I'm so sorry Dad, so sorry."

Didar lay frozen. Could this really be happening? The world he so carefully crafted fell apart. He wasn't perfect, but he'd made great strides in living a good life. Did that not count for anything? He reformed; put his past behind him. He didn't deserve this. Somehow, he found his voice again and surprised himself at how strong and controlled his words flowed.

"I'm sorry you've had to go through this Omar. Trust me, I didn't do this."

Hope returned to Omar's eyes. "I never believed you did, Dad."

But Didar sensed Omar needed to say something else. "What is it, Son? What haven't you told me?"

"I just want to get it all out, Dad. When I submitted my DNA to MyGeneticFamily, a match to a half-sister showed up. I reached out to her, but she didn't respond. When I realized I wasn't a match for you I messaged her again in desperation to find a kidney. She responded and we've been communicating. She suggested I try GENmatch as she refused to be a donor. I didn't understand her unwillingness, but when I told her about the police DNA, she told me her mother was raped and she's a product of that rape." Omar paused. "The good news is she has the same blood type as you and may be a match to donate a kidney." Omar's voice trailed off.

Didar closed his eyes as the ringing in his ears consumed him.

CHAPTER THIRTEEN

The flashlight hung from a string tied to the closet rod casting eerie shadows on the pages of *The Lion, the Witch and the Wardrobe.* Omar loved his closet fort and the flashlight he got for Christmas made it perfect. A comforter softened the sharp edges of toys and shoes lining the floor.

"Have you seen her again?" Omar's mother's voice pierced the closet fort. Heavy eyes widened. He shouldn't listen, but his mother never yelled. Even when he snuck over to Robbie's and returned home an hour later, she didn't yell at him. In fact, she whispered when she asked him to never do it again as she hugged him tighter than ever before. And he never heard his parents argue, until now.

"No, of course not. I left that part of my life behind the minute I met you. I've never seen her again."

The tone of his dad's voice caused shivers to crawl up Omar's spine. He sounded scared. An ache crept into his tummy.

"Then who's been calling and hanging up? And where were you the other night?"

Omar shifted and rolled to his right side, closing his book. With his left arm he folded the pillow over his ear, trying to block out the voices. But even through the pillow his mother's voice continued.

"What are you lying to me about? I can feel it in my bones."

Lying? His dad hated it when people lied. Why would his mom accuse him of such a thing? He didn't lie. The pillow released in time to catch the end of his dad's reply.

"... at work, like I said, helping the accountant with the end of month books. I'm telling the truth, Mahtob. I'd never lie to you. As for who's calling, I have no idea."

Omar sat up and turned the flashlight off. With one foot he pushed on the closet door and it folded outward, turning his fort back into a closet. He tossed the pillow on the bed and tugged at the comforter, but it caught on something. With an extra tug, his book crashed into the door. Omar froze. The voices stopped. He leaped into action; threw his comforter on the bed and grabbed the book placing it on the floor nearby so it appeared to have fallen. Sliding into bed, he pulled the comforter up over his chin and closed his eyes.

The bedroom door opened and someone entered. The book slid onto the nightstand and the door closed.

A much quieter voice from his mother crept through the cracks of his door. "He's sleeping. Looks like a book fell off his bed. I don't think he heard anything."

Sobs tugged at his heart.

"I'd never do anything to jeopardize your trust and the life we've built." His dad's voice still trembled.

Omar laid awake for a long time that night. It never occurred to him his parents might argue. Robbie's mom and dad divorced, but even Omar saw them fighting. His parents weren't like that at all. They were a normal family. A happy family. But the pit of his stomach ached, hinting that not everything was as it seemed.

CHAPTER FOURTEEN

J ahana turned her attention to the restaurant entrance. She glanced at her watch when a man with black hair, and a beard, looking just like his profile picture, entered. The hostess pointed to Jahana, and he strode toward her.

My brother. Jahana slid out of the booth and stood, smoothing her top, tugging at the bottom both front and back. Their eyes met; his smiled. *What does he think of me?*

With a hand raised to his heart he bowed. But she wasn't just any Muslim woman, she was his sister. Her arms reached forward and she enveloped him in a hug. Tentatively he patted her back and gently squeezed. When they released, her eyes stung. She hadn't expected this moment to mean so much. They slid into the booth.

Omar broke the silence. "At last, my sister." He reached across the table and Jahana covered his hand with hers.

"Thank you so much for meeting."

"No, I want to thank you. Flying up to Ottawa, in the winter?" Jahana chuckled. "But seriously, I'm humbled."

Omar waved off her comment. "I'm relieved you still want to meet. I feel like I've known you all my life. You're family."

Jahana smiled. Easing into it was important, but she wanted to get to the point.

"So, Omar, is Didar our biological father?"

The smile left Omar's eyes and he glanced down. Before responding he sighed. "He is." The words, barely audible, screamed in their simplicity.

"Oh Omar, this must be so hard for you." That was all Jahana could manage. Inside she screamed. *How can you sit there and not hate your father? How can you continue to care for someone who's a rapist and a murderer?*

Omar swallowed. "He denies it all. As hard as this might be for you to hear, I believe him. And you would too if you met him. Yes, he did some things in his past that weren't good, but there's no way he did what he's accused of." His voice tapered off and silence followed.

Jahana sighed and stared at the table, running a finger along the edge of the drink coaster. They hadn't even ordered and already a rift formed between them. She remembered the bottle of maple syrup in her purse. It seemed like a stupid idea to bring a gift now. But maybe that's what was needed to break the tension.

She unzipped her purse and handed the syrup to Omar. "It seems like a foolish idea, but I brought you a gift from Ottawa."

"So, what can I get you to drink?" The waitress stood in front of them smiling as if today was the best day she'd ever lived. Neither knew what to say.

Omar spoke first. "Just a coffee for me, thanks."

Jahana ordered a tea. The waitress moved on to the next booth and left them avoiding each other's gaze. Omar's fingers drummed on the table. At last he looked up and Jahana clasped her hands under the table.

"Thank you for the syrup. It's very kind of you. Wish I'd thought to bring you something."

Jahana smiled weakly and silence fell over the table once again.

Omar set the maple syrup on the table between them. "I didn't want to get into this so quickly. I respect your point of view. But my dad is a wonderful man. If you knew him, you'd understand he's not the monster you've made him out to be. You need to meet him."

Jahana's jaw clenched, and she placed her hands on the table. "Omar I'm trying to understand. But do you realize what it's like to find out you're a product of a sexual assault? That your father left your seventeen-year-old mother in an alley to die or be tortured by the regime? Your father cared so little for women he abused her and likely others. And now he denies it?" Jahana stopped. She noticed people at the table across from them staring.

Omar leaned forward, and lowered his voice. "Everyone has their own perspective and time warps that perspective. My dad has always been open about regrets for things he's done in his life. In fact, I recall as a child, conversations where he hinted at how he wasn't a good person, but he worked on trying to be better. I never knew the person he hinted at. He was good to me, to my mother and to anyone else he interacted with. Clearly, your mother has a version of events that took place when you were conceived. My father denies all claims of rape and murder of another woman. I'm asking you to allow him to tell you. Come to New York and meet him. I'll pay for your ticket."

The last thing Jahana wanted was to meet the man who raped her mother. But maybe he needed to face the consequences of his actions. "I'll tell you right now, meeting your father, and yes I call him your father because as far as I'm concerned, he's not a father to me, is the last thing I want to do. But he needs to face what he's done. I bet he can't look me in the eye and tell me he's innocent." She regretted the words as soon as they left her mouth. A glimmer of hope entered Omar's eyes.

"Meeting him would change your mind. You'd understand there are multiple perspectives at play here."

Jahana raised her hand and interrupted. "No, Omar, I can't see there being a possibility of me changing my mind.

The only reason I might meet Didar is to tell him how much I hate him."

Omar smiled. "That's fine Jahana. Whatever your reason, it's important for you to meet. But there's something else too. If he's charged, there's no way he'll get a kidney donation. The list is long. He might not be able to wait till he comes up on the list and a live donor won't step forward when they see his charges. I hope you'll reconsider after you meet him. Did you get tested? Are you a match?"

Jahana slumped in her chair. She'd hoped it wouldn't be all about the pitch. But Omar came to save his father. She was his ticket. It would be easy to refuse again, but until she met Didar, she wouldn't be able to make a definitive decision to withhold another person's opportunity to live. The irony of the situation didn't evade her. He'd given her life, left her mother to die and now the responsibility of returning life to him fell on her.

Jahana sighed, and nodded.

****

"She's a match, Dad. And she wants to meet you." Omar barely contained himself. After all the bad news, having something good to talk about was a relief.

Didar's eyes flashed. "What? Omar, I never asked you to do any of this. I don't want to meet her. Don't bring her here." Didar kicked the sheets off himself.

Omar's face flushed. He hadn't expected this reaction. Didn't he want to live? Surely, he could see how finding his daughter could save his life? "Now Dad, calm down..."

"Don't tell me to calm down. I don't want to meet someone who hates me and believes things that aren't true! I may have been a careless, entitled young man with hormones, but I didn't rape anyone."

"And that's what you need to tell Jahana. She needs to hear your side of the story." Omar took a breath. "Dad, she can save your life. And she's your daughter. She's agreed to meet you. Doesn't she have a right to the truth to understand what happened?"

The anger in Didar's eyes subsided.

Omar let him process the words before continuing. "What is it you're really worried about?"

Didar's eyes welled up with tears and he turned his head away. The large wall clock ticked off the seconds. A cart rattled by the partially closed door and the chatter of voices at the nursing station floated down the hall sliding around the door into the room. Omar waited for a response. As much as he wanted to fill the air with words, clutter the space between them, he didn't want to take away his dad's opportunity to open up and tell him what really bothered him.

Didar coughed and pushed himself up in bed. "Omar, it's your mother. I don't want to hurt her. She doesn't know about Jahana. Mahtob has forgiven relations I had before we met, absolved my transgressions. But Jahana coming into our lives may be more than she's willing to put up with."

Omar hadn't considered the implications to his parents' relationship. "But Dad, Mom wants you to live. She'll be grateful there's someone who can donate a kidney."

"But she's only coming to meet me. What if she decides not to donate after we talk? This will all be for nothing. I'll put Mahtob through this for no reason." Didar leaned forward. "It's not worth the risk of losing your mother."

Omar raised his hands. "Okay, okay I understand. But Dad, would knowing about Jahana make Mom walk out when she's stayed by your side after your accusations of rape and murder?" It came out more direct than he would have liked, but it seemed so obvious to Omar. His parents loved each other. A long-lost daughter showing up now really shouldn't be a worry. "You did tell Mom about the DNA test results from the samples I took, didn't you?"

Didar nodded and tapped his foot on the floor. "Jahana's presence makes everything more tangible. Her mother's accusations might hold more meaning for Mahtob. What if it's the final straw for her? I just can't chance it."

Omar clenched his teeth. "Are you kidding Dad? Jahana can save your life and Mom wants you to live. Talk to her and explain you have a daughter. Jahana's willing to visit and you'll not ruin this opportunity for her to get to meet the man I know; a great father and a doting husband. The values you've taught are good values to live by. She needs to see the real Didar, not the one that's morphed into a monster through the imagination of a woman who got pregnant and needed to explain her situation. Don't you agree, Dad? She had to explain her pregnancy and so made you out to be a villain." Omar played the diplomat long enough. "It seems likely a Jewish girl in Tehran explained her pregnancy in a way that wouldn't get her in trouble with her family. Rape was a perfect alibi."

"Don't go there Omar. It's not for us to judge her situation. But I don't remember this woman, and while I sewed a few oats in my time, I didn't rape anyone. I also drank a lot in my younger days and don't always remember what I did, but rape wasn't in my repertoire. Two accusations of rape, however, may be more than your mother can take. I need to talk to her about Jahana. Just give me some time to figure out how to bring it up."

Omar breathed a sigh of relief. "Okay Dad, but we have little time to play with. I don't want Jahana to change her mind about coming. Can you talk to Mom this week?"

"Just like your old man, relentless."

The corner of Didar's mouth hinted at a smile, but the troubled look in his eyes made Omar doubt his grin.

"I'll do my best, Son."

****

Three days after taking the official samples, the police called on Didar to tell him he was a suspect in their cold case. They weren't charging him yet, but advised him not to leave town.

Mahtob became quieter, didn't stay as long at the hospital and when she was there, she avoided eye contact. When Didar explained his innocence, she nodded and hugged him like she believed his side of the story. But things changed, and he didn't want to ask her what bothered her. And now he needed to add to her anguish.

The sunlight entering the room seemed to slow down as he adjusted his position and prepared to confront Mahtob with the fact he had a daughter.

"Mahtob, honey, I need to talk to you about something."

Her eyes snapped to meet his.

A sad, hot feeling welled up in Didar. Not that long ago, she would have smiled at his reference to 'honey', but with all the surprises she'd endured lately, she put up a defence as soon as he said the word.

"Remember how Omar had his DNA tested before I landed in the hospital and how he's since posted his results to GENmatch?"

Mahtob rolled her eyes. It wasn't the best start to the conversation. Of course, she knew, she'd learned about it when he explained the reason the police suspected him of rape and murder.

"Now what Didar? What else has your past come to collect?" Regret filled her eyes as soon as the words left her mouth. But they hung on the tension in the air, waiting for his response.

He cleared his throat, and lowered his eyes as he struggled to find the right words. He took a slow breath before speaking. "Well, Omar failed to tell us he matched to someone when he received his initial results. Her name is Jahana, and she's a half-sister to Omar."

Mahtob's mouth opened and closed twice before words escaped the fury she held inside. "A sister? You have a daughter with another woman?"

Didar scrambled to do damage control. He swung his legs over the side of the bed and stood, reaching out and grabbing Mahtob's hand. She backed up and swatted his hand away.

"I swear I knew nothing about this person until Didar told me last week. I've been wanting to tell you, but I don't want to hurt you more than I already have. It happened before we married. Before I came to America. Before you changed my life. Before I loved you." Didar's voice quieted to a whisper.

Mahtob stood still, and he moved forward again, grasping her shoulders as he gazed into her eyes. He hadn't even told her the worst part.

"Where does she live? What's her name?"

At least she isn't dismissing her.

"In Canada. Ottawa. So not far."

"Does she want to meet you?"

Didar tried to gauge her reaction before he replied. What difference would it make to her if Jahana wanted to visit him?

"Yes. Omar told me she plans to come meet me. Mahtob, she's a match to be a kidney donor."

A flash of relief passed over Mahtob's face. While fleeting, Didar held on to it.

"She hasn't yet agreed to be a donor. She wants to meet me first."

Didar could see the puzzled look on Mahtob's face. "So, is her mother coming with her? Has Omar also been in touch with her?"

"No, no, not at all." He responded quickly, perhaps too quickly.

"So, who is Jahana's mother, Didar?"

"Now Mahtob, this is going to sound terrible and I want you to remember the person I am today is not who I was back then. You know that right?" Didar searched for some kind of sign. Something to tell him she remembered he'd changed when she came into his life. But she stood quietly, no emotions crossing her face.

"Okay, so I don't remember her. I had a bit of a wild streak as a young man and she was a victim of that era. If I'd known she was pregnant I would have helped her, I swear. I would have owned up to my responsibilities. But she never sought me out."

Didar couldn't tell if this consoled Mahtob or angered her more, but he knew what he was about to say next would definitely make her mad. "So, I'm sorry Mahtob, but there's more." Before she could interject, he continued. "Jahana's mother claims I raped her, and Jahana was a product of that rape."

The air left the room, perhaps sucked into Mahtob's lungs as she inhaled sharply.

Didar stepped toward her, hands up between them. "Now I know what you're thinking. Two different accusations of rape? It must be true. But I swear Mahtob, it's not. The past is not coming to collect what's owed. My wild days morphed into something else coming back to ruin a good life." Didar paused not sure if he should bring up Omar's theory or not, but the anger in Mahtob's eyes made him decide to use it to his advantage. "Omar has concluded Jahana's mother made up her story because she got pregnant and needed an alibi. I'm not pretending I'm innocent. You know I had sex a few times in my younger days, but it was always consensual. I raped no one." Didar continued to grip Mahtob's shoulders.

"And this girl wants to meet you? If she believes she's a product of a sexual assault, why would she want to meet you? Why would she even consider donating a kidney to you?" Mahtob's eyes brimmed with tears.

"Omar says he's talked to Jahana and told her I'm not the man she thinks I am. As for the kidney, she hasn't committed to donate it; in fact, she probably won't. But Omar can convince anybody to do things they don't want to do. He's convinced her to come meet me and see I'm not the monster her mother talks about."

"Sorry Didar, I need to process this." Mahtob backed out of Didar's grip, picked her purse up off the chair and folded her jacket over her arm.

"But Mahtob, the home dialysis training session starts soon. If you leave, you'll miss it."

Mahtob paused. "I'm sorry, we'll have to do it another day." Mahtob turned and walked out of the hospital room.

CHAPTER FIFTEEN

❧

Two weeks ago, Omar doubted this would ever happen, but it did. Jahana boarded a plane in Ottawa and he agreed to pick her up at JFK in an hour.

Have a good flight. See you soon.

Omar hoped Jahana hadn't turned her phone to airplane mode.

A text response appeared right away.

Things don't look good. There's a raging storm and although this flight isn't cancelled, most are. We're delayed two hours.

Omar slammed his fist on the counter.

Damn. Of all the days for a storm, did it have to hit today?

Didar had agreed to meet Jahana. Mahtob declined the invitation. After his dad told her about Jahana, Mahtob seemed more subdued. His DNA testing had turned her world on its head. If Brie dumped something like this on him, he wasn't sure he'd be so understanding. But then again, they didn't have over 30 years of history like his parents did.

Brie still lived at Kathy's apartment. They saw each other most days, and she seemed content. Happier than she had when they lived together. What if she never moved back? His father brought added baggage to the relationship; a father charged with rape and murder wasn't an easy thing to live with. And he discussed everything with her. Without her he'd have drowned long ago.

Omar drove to the office and immersed himself in paperwork. Two hours later, Jahana sent another text.

So, we're boarding. We need to de-ice, so I'm not sure when we'll arrive. Can you keep checking arrival times? I don't want you waiting at the airport.

Sure will. Glad the plane is leaving soon. Safe travels. See you at this end.

Omar glanced out of his office window. The snow came down heavy there too. He'd have to leave soon as it might take him as long to get to the airport as it would for Jahana to fly in.

He cleared a couple emails from his inbox and checked the flight status. Still hadn't taken off, but he imagined they'd be in a big queue to get de-iced. Then his phone vibrated again.

"We deplaned. They cancelled the flight. I won't be going anywhere today."

Omar picked up the phone and called. "Oh Jahana, I'm so sorry! Damn weather. Can you try again tomorrow?"

"I'm afraid not Omar. I have midterms coming up for my students. It'll be at least a month now before I can get away again. I'll check my schedule and get back to you."

Omar heard relief in Jahana's voice. It took a lot for her to commit to a visit. This would give her more time to talk herself out of it.

"Well, whenever it's convenient for you, I'll book another flight."

"Thanks Omar. Sorry this didn't work out."

****

As Jahana climbed into the taxi, she wondered whether the universe was sending signs. Maybe she shouldn't meet her father. Needing to wait another month wasn't exactly true. She wanted to buy some time to think things through. It would be so easy to not try again. Why did she feel the need to meet the man who raped her mother and murdered and raped another woman? She shook her head. No need to get involved.

But she'd already committed. When she replied to Omar's message, she became involved. She liked Omar, and he made her want to meet Didar. He intrigued her. How could this man be a monster on one hand and a wonderful father on the other?

Jahana flipped to her contacts on her phone. Maybe she should discuss this with her mother. Her thumb hesitated, hovering. They had a few conversations, but she hadn't mentioned finding a half brother or the fact she found her biological father. Would it open a wound that had healed or heal a wound that remained raw? And she'd have to tell her about the charges against him. She couldn't imagine her mother encouraging her to meet Didar. So, what was the point in bringing it up? There wasn't any.

The taxi crawled through deserted streets, pushing bumper height accumulated snow. The snow pelted sideways. As they turned into her street slight indents where tires once tread hours ago were the only signs she was not alone in the world. It felt like everyone had hibernated from winter's thrust. Now, that seemed like a good idea. She unlocked the front door entering the quiet interior and stamped her feet. Mounds of snow transformed into puddles.

Her muscles ached and her head throbbed, but she poured a cup of tea and folded herself into the La-Z-Boy recliner. She gazed out at the storm and reached behind her, steadying her cup with her left hand, and pulled the blanket off the back of the chair. A shiver escaped her lips as she tucked it in and pulled it up to her chin, leaving only her tea hand exposed to the frigid air.

As she watched the snow falling, she remembered something she read somewhere about mercy being a muscle. A muscle you needed to exercise or, like any other muscle, it cramps up. Was she exercising her mercy muscle? Showing her father mercy by visiting him? But would she give him false hope? Would he think she might donate a kidney? She had no intention of doing that. So, no this wasn't a mercy mission; curiosity plain and simple. Who was the monster Omar loved? Where did Omar's blind spot come from? She wanted to stand in front of this man and make him quiver. Face his past. Atone for his sins.

The snow swirled, and Jahana made a decision. She'd make him accountable. That's really what she wanted. But could she tell him she wouldn't save his life? His life was in her hands. If she withheld her kidney would she be stooping to his level?

Jahana rubbed her temples and raised the tea cup to finish the last mouthful. She hadn't eaten for hours and the caffeine spurred her on. She'd go to New York and meet her father. But it would be on her terms. No need to tell Omar. With Didar in the hospital, no one else needed to know. She wouldn't have to go to his home or meet his wife. She could just show up at the hospital. Whether or not the visit went well would be between the two of them. No one else needed to know if they decided that's the way they wanted it. It would be a safe place to confront him.

The girls were staying with her dad until Sunday. She could catch a flight Saturday morning and be back that night. No sense trying to go tomorrow, the cancelled flights from today would just cause chaos at the airport.

One phone call and an hour later, the plans were in motion. She'd leave at 7:00 am Saturday, weather permitting, and return late afternoon. This was it. She would do this. With a quick rinse of the cup she climbed the stairs to bed, exhausted.

CHAPTER SIXTEEN

"You bastard!"

Omar's eyes widened. After he turned twenty-one, Didar took him on a business trip. So far it hadn't been much fun, meetings after meetings. Tonight, they returned to the hotel late and opted for the hotel bar instead of a restaurant.

The woman stood in front of them, hands on her hips. Her salt and pepper hair accentuated her blue eyes, stunning. Her crows-feet gave away her age and Omar assumed her interest was likely in his dad. Didar always commanded attention, but not this kind.

Omar sat rooted to the barstool as her expensive martini flew from her glass into his dad's face. She slammed the glass down on the counter and wheeled around to leave. Didar sat motionless, sadness clouding his face. Perhaps a flicker of recognition?

"Whoa, not so fast," Omar called out. He rose and strode after her, but his dad grabbed his arm and held it tight.

"Dad, she can't get away with that." Omar struggled to release his dad's grip, to no avail.

"Let her go, Omar. I didn't earn her anger, but if there's one thing I've learned, there's no sense arguing with an angry woman." The corners of his mouth broke into a grin.

Omar stared at his dad through narrow eyes. *A woman just tossed a drink in his face and he cracked jokes?*

"Who is she?"

Didar glanced sideways at the bar door, closing behind her before responding. "Never seen her in my life, Son." *She has me confused with someone else.* Didar used his free hand to mop his face with a stack of napkins provided by the bartender.

"She needs to know she can't go around tossing drinks in men's faces and walk away." Omar grabbed his dad's hand and pulled free from his grip.

"Omar, that's enough. Just leave her," Didar barked. The edge to his father's voice stopped him. One glance at his dad's face and he knew better than to question his resolve.

Omar returned to the barstool. He'd looked forward to tonight. And now a lunatic's actions overshadowed his first drink in a bar with his dad. Twenty-one came with its perks, but seeing his dad assaulted and then do nothing about it wasn't one of them.

Didar cleared his throat and wiped the last of the liquid off his chin before loosening his tie. "Maybe it'll save the other guy from getting that treatment. No sense both of us experiencing her wrath." Didar gave a half-hearted chuckle before tipping back his bourbon to drain the glass. He motioned for the bartender to pour each of them another.

"Does this happen to you often," Omar teased, a niggle of worry tucked away in the folds of his brain. He too threw back his bourbon.

"Can't say it does. This would be a first. Sorry you were here to see it." Didar's eyes grew serious for a moment and then sparkled with laughter. Omar couldn't tell if the incident disturbed or amused him.

The bartender set the drinks down and leaned in close. "These are on the house," he grinned and winked, establishing himself as one of the brotherhood.

"Boy I'd hate to be the real guy who wronged her. But what if you run into her again? You don't want a repeat. I wish you'd let me talk to her." Omar swirled the ice in his glass, the amber liquid eddied in the glass's bottom.

"I imagine if I run into her again, she'll realize I'm not who she thought and there'll be no need to set her straight."

Omar raised an eyebrow and considered his dad's perspective. But earlier, when the woman sat across from them, she studied them. She had lots of time to recognize his dad. Mistaken identity made little sense.

"Hope you're right." He dropped the subject.

****

The next morning Omar rose early and headed to the hotel gym. He eyed the three hydraulic weight benches and chose the lone treadmill to help him get through the rest of the day in a boardroom chair. If nothing else, he had a great view of the harbour as he pounded out the miles.

Just as he finished up and turned to leave, the door opened and the woman from the night before entered. They both froze. Omar noted the defiance and anger reflected in her face; not the shame or embarrassment he expected.

Omar broke the stalemate first and didn't mince words. His anger from the night before still festered. "Hey, you're the woman who threw a drink on my dad last night at the bar. Why on earth would you do that?"

She flicked her dark hair over her shoulder and adjusted the strap of her sports bra peeking out beneath her cropped tank top. "Retribution young man. Simple retribution. Your dad deserves more than he got."

Omar glanced around the room, glad the only other person present wore headphones and rocked it out to some loud music. "I think you targeted the wrong man. My dad said he doesn't know you. You owe him an apology."

The woman opened her mouth to speak and spit flew. "First, he's the right man. I'd recognize that face anywhere. And as for an apology. Are you kidding? I have nothing to apologize for. In fact, even if he apologized to me, I'd still have to throw my drink in his face."

Omar stood frozen to the spot. He didn't know how to convince her she had the wrong man. Finally, he blurted out, "What's the man's name you have issues with?"

The woman stopped. The furrow in her brow from years of worry deepened. "Hmm, don't have the luxury of that answer. When he assaulted me, he never mentioned his name. Funny how jerks like that don't disclose their identity. But that face, I'll never forget that face."

Omar let out a nervous chuckle. "Well apparently you've forgotten 'that' face, because my dad could never be the person you're describing." Omar stormed out of the room wishing the door's soft close hinges would slam.

Her last words escaped into the hallway after him. "That's it, honey, bury your head in the sand just like your dad. Pretend it never happened."

CHAPTER SEVENTEEN

Omar set his phone down without bothering to leave another message. He stared out the window deep in thought.

"What's up?" Brie crept up behind him and rested her chin on his shoulder.

She spent a lot of time at the apartment lately. Tonight, she insisted on making dinner and told him to take some time to relax. But he couldn't relax.

"I've been trying to reach Jahana all day, but she's not picking up. I'm afraid she's changed her mind about meeting Dad. If she doesn't meet him, she'll never reconsider donating her kidney."

Brie strode around the sofa and perched herself on the arm sliding her legs across Omar. She cupped his face in her hands. "Listen to me. Give her some space. She'll come around. It was just yesterday her flight was cancelled. If you keep nagging, you'll drive her away."

Omar lifted her legs and rose from the couch. "You're right, but she's slipping away. We need her. Dad needs her."

Brie grabbed his hand. "You've done everything you can. Just let it rest for tonight, please." Her eyes implored him to stay. "Let's eat, dinner's ready."

Omar dropped her hand and headed for his study. "I'll be right there." He heard Brie's exasperated sigh as he exited the room.

Maybe Jahana sent him a message via the MyGeneticFamily app. He flipped on the computer screen. A quick scan revealed no new messages.

What was he doing? His father's kidney consumed him. Perhaps a diversion to avoid thinking about the impending charges? He'd rather focus on the potential of something good. And besides, if he didn't get a kidney there wouldn't be much sense worrying about charges. They'd become a moot point.

The sound of plates being pulled from the cupboard drifted down the hall. If he didn't start being more present around Brie, he'd lose her too. A shudder travelled through his body, remembering when she moved out of the apartment. He wanted and needed her back.

He turned off the monitor and sauntered into the kitchen. Brie stiffened. The aroma of basil and thyme caused his stomach to rumble.

"I'm sorry Brie. I'll try to quit obsessing about Jahana. I appreciate you being here, I really do. I'd be a wreck without you."

Brie turned toward him. Tears filled her eyes and threatened to spill over. "I feel helpless. I want to make all of this go away, but I can't. And you're growing away from me."

Omar opened his mouth to interject, but she held up a hand, to stop him.

"Part of that is my fault. I moved out. But I've had lots of time to think about things and I…"

"Please don't." He placed a finger on her lips. "I'll be better, I promise." Omar's heart raced, and he searched her eyes for answers.

"And I've decided I want to move back in." A smile laced with sadness crept across Brie's face.

"What?" Omar couldn't have hidden the joy in his voice if he'd tried. "You mean it?"

She tossed her head back and gazed into his eyes.

"I mean it. I've been wearing this all night long, but you're too preoccupied to notice." She dangled her left hand in front of him.

He grabbed her by the waist and twirled her, then set her down and stepped back. "Oh Brie, you've just made me the happiest man alive. I can't wait to tell the world we're engaged!" Omar stepped toward her and placed his lips on hers. Her breath quickened. He lifted her onto the counter.

"No, not here," she whispered.

He carried her to the bedroom. Dinner could wait.

****

"Do you swear you've not assaulted any women?" Mahtob sat on the edge of the bed. The morning sun streamed in the window creating a halo behind her. She held his gaze. There was no escaping her. Nor did he want to. The time had come to clear the air and remove her doubt.

"I swear Mahtob." Didar searched her eyes. Did she believe him?

Mahtob paused and seemed to be considering his words. Did she weigh them against all they had been through together?

"Your past is piling up on you. Two accusations of rape, one of murder, an illegitimate daughter. It all seems a bit too much." Mahtob rose from the bed and turned to stare out the window.

"You're right. Such a coincidence that two accusations of rape and a murder come to light right now. And a daughter? Well, I'm blindsided by that too."

Mahtob wheeled around. "I'm not upset you have a daughter, but I'm upset her mother claims you sexually assaulted her. Didar, that's two women. How many more are there?" Mahtob's voice caught, her eyes brimmed with tears.

"There's no explanation other than to say I didn't rape or murder anyone. It was a long time ago. A different time. Can we put today's lens on what happened back then? Perspectives change. I had consensual sex more than I'd like to admit back in the day. And I wasn't the most considerate lover, but I didn't rape or murder anyone. As for Jahana, she's my daughter but her conception was not by a sexual assault."

Mahtob choked on her anguish. "You told me about your transgressions when I first met you, but what about Lana? She was here when I stopped by the other day. And she sent roses! We both know what roses mean and she does too."

Didar stood at the side of his bed and reached for her hand, but she backed away. "Listen, I can't control what women say or do. All I can do is tell the truth. And the truth is there's nothing going on between Lana and me. If she has some kind of infatuation, I can't help that. But I've never strayed, I swear. You're the only woman I've ever loved and I'd never jeopardize our relationship. Please believe me."

Didar stepped ahead and this time Mahtob moved towards him, cheeks streaked with tears, the light of acceptance in her eyes. She reached out and circled him in her arms. They rocked side to side. He inhaled her scent. If he was a religious man, he'd believe she was heaven sent. Without her he'd be nothing more than a shell. She made him whole, and he worked at being a better man every single day.

As she pulled away, her words surprised him. "I never want to meet her, Didar. Jahana can't become part of our lives. If she needs to meet you that's fine, but I don't want to be part of it. I couldn't bear to hear her lies about you. She may be the one person who can save your life, but I will not be telling her how grateful I am."

Didar bowed his head. "Okay Mahtob, there should be no reason for you to have to meet. I don't know what I can say to convince her I'm not the monster she thinks I am. So, I doubt she'll be willing to donate a kidney."

"Well, I hope she does Didar." Mahtob sighed.

"But how can I let her donate a body part to me, no matter how old she is? It seems wrong. She's young. She might need that kidney herself someday." Didar paused thinking about how he'd insisted Omar not donate a kidney. If he couldn't take one from Omar, why would he be able to take one from Jahana?

But things had changed a lot since he thought Omar could donate. If he'd known he would be up on charges of rape and murder, maybe he wouldn't have dismissed Omar's potential kidney either. Maybe he could accept a kidney from Jahana because she didn't feel like his daughter.

"You'd better consider it if she offers. We may not get another." Mahtob's eyes flashed.

Didar sighed. She was right. But Jahana had no good reason to meet him. Even if she showed up, what would make her want to donate a kidney to him?

"Alright Mr. and Mrs. Fassid, let's go for your training." The orderly blew into the room with a wheel chair.

Didar looked over the top of his glasses at him.

"Now Mr. Fassid. It's a long walk. If you want to be on your game when you get there, I suggest you strap in and let me wheel you down."

Didar rolled his eyes but sat down and let himself be wheeled out of the room and into the elevator.

****

The dialysis training turned out to be easier than he expected. They both felt comfortable. One more day and he might go home.

Mahtob leaned over to place a kiss on his cheek. "I'll see you tomorrow. Anything else you want me to bring? Sounds like we should be able to take you home about noon."

"Just the coat and boots. I can't wait to sleep in our bed, together."

Mahtob squeezed his hand before striding to the door. She turned and smiled before escaping down the hall.

As Mahtob retreated, Didar noticed a woman standing across the hall. Waiting. She watched Mahtob. He heard the elevator door open and Mahtob's footsteps disappear inside. The woman across the hall glanced at her phone then straightened and headed towards his room.

****

Jahana obtained the room number from the information booth in the lobby. She stood across the hall outside Didar's room and watched, who she assumed must be Didar and a woman. His wife? When she first arrived, they seemed to argue. She couldn't make out the words and didn't want to. Then they made up and left together with someone from the hospital. She hoped he'd return alone. But she came back too. Jahana glanced at her watch; two o'clock. Her flight left at five. She tapped her foot, her back resting against the wall as she scrolled through messages on her phone. Omar had sent her several messages that she ignored; not wanting him to figure out her plans.

A few minutes later, the woman walked out of the room and onto the elevator. Her phone vibrated, Omar again. She slid the phone back into her pocket and stepped forward. Time to introduce herself.

He watched her walk across the hall. Had he guessed who she was? She paused at the door.

"Can I come in?"

Didar smiled and gestured for her to enter. He had a nice smile. One of those smiles that draws you in, insists you like them. Omar had it too.

"Certainly. Do I know you?" Didar cocked his head and searched her face for some kind of clue.

134

"Thank you." Jahana walked halfway into the room and stood, shifting her weight from one foot to the other. She prepared a speech, but none of it seemed appropriate now. "Um, please don't get upset, you're not supposed to get upset, but I…" Her voice trailed off. She coughed a little and continued. "I'm Jahana, your… daughter."

The speech replayed in her mind hundreds of times over the last few days. How would he react? She expected surprise or anger or taunting. But instead his face lit up, and he sat up in bed, swinging his legs over the side, then reached out to shake hands.

His hand felt warm and smooth. No callouses or rough spots. She searched his eyes, trying to read his thoughts.

His other hand rested on top of hers and with sincerity, like she'd never heard before, simply said, "So nice to meet you Jahana. So very nice indeed."

She pulled away. This wasn't how she envisioned their meeting. There was a reason she came all this way. She'd make him realize what a monster he really was. She would not be sidetracked from the real reason for the visit.

He stepped back and motioned to the chair at the foot of the bed. "Please have a seat. There's lots for us to talk about." He settled back into bed, adjusting the head of the bed so he sat upright.

Jahana perched on the chair. Not because he told her to, but because her knees became very weak and her feet throbbed. She should have worn more comfortable shoes, but she dressed to impress, not to be comfortable.

"Before you start, feel free to ask me anything. There's a lot of misunderstanding between us and I want to fix that."

I'm sure you do. You're a snake. He'd gotten away with everything by being charming.

"Was that your wife that just left?" Jahana's voice trailed off.

"Yes, Omar's mother, Mahtob." He spoke Mahtob's name softly, with reverence.

Jahana cleared her throat. "I don't have much time, so I hope you don't mind if we get to the point of my visit. I'm heading back on the 5 o'clock to Ottawa. Omar isn't aware I'm here. In fact, no one knows." She halted. Should she tell someone who might be charged with murder that no one knew she'd come? She needed to get back on track.

"Oh, that's too bad. I'd like to spend more time with you."

Jahana jumped in. The spell he created evaporated. "Well, you won't get more time. In fact, this is the only time you'll get." She hadn't planned to be adversarial and regretted the words as soon as they left her lips.

Didar turned away and stared out the window. "I see. I can understand how you'd feel that way."

"Do you though?" Her voice caught. She would not be angry. Just factual. She moved the chair closer and leaned forward. "Listen, I didn't come here to get angry or get any justification from you for your actions. I came here for

Omar. And if I'm honest, a bit for myself. I needed to meet the man I could donate a kidney to, but won't."

Didar turned back to face her. The pain in his face could be felt in the pit of her stomach.

"Thank you for coming. I'm not sure I would've done the same in your situation. You're an amazing person. Thank you for letting me meet you."

Jahana expected excuses and denials. But he wasn't doing that. Did this change anything?

"So, you raped my mother? You're not embarrassed to look at me, a product of your sexual assault? Living proof of what you did?" Jahana practically spit out the last words. Heat rose in her cheeks.

His jaw worked back and forth. Somehow, he'd aged since she entered the room. Tempting as it was to keep talking and put everything on the table, she waited for his response.

His voice shook. "You're living proof I had sex with your mother. We can agree all children play that role. And no, I'm not embarrassed to look at you. You're a fine woman, that's clear. If your mother and I didn't have sex, you wouldn't be here. And I can see that would be a travesty."

"So, you admit you raped her?"

"Now Jahana, you won't like to hear this, but I don't remember your mother. As a young man in Tehran, I was privileged and took advantage of my status. I slept with a lot of women, but I can assure you it was always consensual."

Jahana's anger bubbled up again, and she forced it down. In a quiet voice she muttered, "You're telling me my mother is lying?"

"I'm telling you your mother and I have different perspectives. I'm not proud of the fact I don't remember your mother and she could be one of dozens of women I slept with during that wild period of my life. And..." Didar paused. "The women I had sex with liked it rough." Didar's voice trailed off and then he added, "And so did I."

Jahana sat in silence, too stunned to respond. He thought rape was rough sex? "And what about the cold case? The police have listed you as a suspect for rape and murder. Is that a difference in perception too?"

Didar's face flushed. She'd hit a nerve. "No, I mean, yes. I mean I never raped or murdered anyone. It looks bad, but I didn't."

Jahana took a deep breath. She didn't come here to get his blood pressure up. "Okay, I can see you believe what you're saying. Please take a breath and lean back."

Jahana waited a couple of minutes while Didar closed his eyes. She glanced at her watch, two forty-five. She'd need to leave soon.

His eyes opened and his colour returned to normal.

"Didar, I came here to tell you I won't donate a kidney. I believe you did the things you're accused of and you don't deserve a kidney when so many other people do."

Didar nodded in agreement. "I could never ask that of you, anyway."

They sat in silence. Was there anything left to say? As she sat glaring at an old man in a hospital bed, surrounded by white walls and gleaming floors, she thought of the cold case victim's family. If he died, they'd never get closure. They might never find out what happened to their daughter, sister, maybe mother? Closure was within her power. She could make him pay for what he'd done. *I won't let you take the easy way out and die before facing your truth.*

"Didar, something just occurred to me." Jahana paused before proceeding. "I may have a deal you can't refuse."

****

As Omar approached his dad's hospital room, excited at the prospect of announcing his engagement to Brie, voices reached him, and he stopped. It wasn't his mother's voice drifting down the hall, but it sounded familiar. Then he realized, Jahana. His stomach flipped. Why had she shown up unannounced? As much as he wanted to burst into the room and confront her, the next thing he heard stopped him from venturing further.

"It's occurred to me that if you die before charges are laid and you go to trial, the family of the victim will never get closure. At the same time, a trial may drag out details and visuals that family should never have to live with. What if I donate a kidney to you on one condition?"

Omar held his breath. This was more than he could have hoped for.

"You tell the police you raped and murdered that woman in their cold case and I'll donate my kidney." If Omar could have moved, he would have. But he stood motionless, his jaw open. How could she be so kind and so cruel at the same time?

Omar strained to hear his dad's reply. "Why would you want me to do that?"

"To give closure to the family of the murdered woman, without them having to endure the horrors of a trial. If I can give that to the family, it's worth donating a kidney."

Omar remained motionless, too invested to leave or interrupt. What would his father say?

"But I didn't do it. I'm innocent."

Omar slumped forward, a deep sigh escaping. Any doubts he had about his father's innocence evaporated.

"Are you sure about that? Do you want to stick to that story, or do you want to live?"

He would never have guessed this side of Jahana existed.

A long period of silence preceded Didar's answer. When he spoke up, anger and resignation filled his voice. "If they charge me, I'll plead guilty. You've got a deal."

Omar covered his mouth as a guttural groan escaped. He turned toward the elevator, unable to face either his sister or his father. How could Jahana ask such a thing and how could his dad agree? This was not what he expected. If he moderated the conversation, it would have turned out differently. Who did she think she was coming to see his dad without telling anyone?

Omar exited the elevator into the lobby of the hospital. The gift shop invited visitors to his right. The smell of flowers wafted across the lobby. Why did so many people sit in the lobby? Why wouldn't they either be visiting someone or leaving? It was something he could never understand. At last he eyed a seat on a bench in a back corner and positioned himself to watch the elevator. What would he do when he spotted her? His body vibrated, his fists clenched and unclenched.

Jahana strode off the elevator a few minutes later. Her eyes darted around the lobby before she reached into her purse. Her steps quickened. Had something transpired after Omar left? She stared at her phone

He strode toward her, then paused. What would he say? She was giving his dad a kidney. How could he jeopardize that? Without moving he watched her walk out the front doors.

I'm a damn coward. I should have confronted her. But in his heart Omar needed to think this through. Too much was at stake.

He turned back toward the elevator and put his game face on. He'd wait for Didar to tell him about the deal and pretend he hadn't heard their conversation.

As he approached the room, he ran his hand through his hair and took a deep breath.

"Hey Dad. How's it going?" Words spilled out of his mouth before he realized there was no one in the room. The toilet flushed in the bathroom. He settled into the chair and waited.

His dad shuffled to his bed; a crease worn deep in his forehead. He didn't notice Omar sitting at the foot of the bed.

"Hey Dad, how's it going?" This time it came out less enthusiastically and with more trepidation.

"Omar!" The creases in his forehead disappeared, and a smile lit his face.

"You're looking good," Omar lied. "Feeling okay today?"

"I'm great. You'll never believe who just left." Didar paused like Omar was supposed to play a guessing game, but Omar just stared waiting for his answer.

"Jahana."

Omar rifled through the list of reactions he'd rehearsed on the way up the elevator. "What? Really? She said she couldn't come for a month?" He hoped he mustered enough surprise in his response.

"Yeah, she said she just decided to fly down and back the same day. Too bad you missed her; she just left."

"So how did it go? How's your blood pressure?"

"Oh, fine, fine. We had a nice talk. Got to know each other a little. She didn't have much time. But Omar, you'll never believe it. She offered to donate a kidney!"

Omar paused, waiting to hear the rest of the story. But it became clear the deal would remain a secret.

"What? Are you kidding? She was so adamant she wouldn't donate her kidney. How did you change her mind?" Omar choked on the last question. Maybe he convinced Jahana he didn't have to plead guilty?

"I'm not sure. Must have been my charm." Didar smiled as only he could.

"That's incredible news, Dad! I can't believe it. You'll get a kidney." Omar jumped to his feet and hugged Didar. *Come on Dad, when are you going to reveal the rest of the story?*

Omar held his dad at shoulder's length. Didar fought back tears, breaking Omar's hold and becoming interested in straightening the sheets on the bed. Omar let him. He'd have to be patient and wait for him to reveal the deal when he was ready.

"Things are coming together, Dad, Mom texted to say one more day and you'll be going home. I'll get in touch with your doctor and see what we need to do for the transplant. I'll call Jahana to be sure everything runs smoothly from her end. This is exciting Dad. Everything's falling into place. You'll see. We'll put it all behind us. Once you get your kidney, we'll deal with this other thing if it amounts to anything. It's going to be okay." Omar wished he could read his dad's expression, but he continued to tuck in the sheets, not glancing in Omar's direction.

"One step at a time, Son. One step at a time."

****

Omar waited until he reached the car before he exploded. The palm of his hand hit the dash until a shooting pain radiated from his wrist to his elbow. He leaned forward resting his head on his arms cradling the steering wheel. If he hadn't overheard their conversation, he'd be ecstatic. Jahana decided to donate a kidney. His dad would live. But if the police laid charges, he'd be living in jail.

Why didn't his dad say anything about Jahana's ultimatum? Did he convince her otherwise? A trial would be better than pleading guilty. Better yet, no charges would take care of everything.

Focus. One thing at a time. He needed to get their lawyer up to speed, just in case the charges came through. It was a catch twenty-two. Face charges with a trial and maybe be a free man with a death sentence or plead guilty and live incarcerated for the rest of his life. His hands were tied. Didar was stubborn, he'd do what he wanted. It would be difficult to change his mind. Omar had to focus on what he could do: facilitate the kidney transplant by helping his dad and Jahana through the paperwork. Omar couldn't do anything about the deal, if there was a deal. No sense worrying about something that might not even exist.

Omar strode into the apartment and headed down the hall to the study. A friend of his went to court for a trumped-up case of assault. His lawyer got him off. He'd start there. A quick google search and he found the firm, Frank Jesperson and Associates.

When the phone rang through to voicemail, Omar glanced at his watch, five thirty. The office was closed. How do you leave a voicemail about this? He paused and then hung up. How do you say, "hey my dad is a suspect in a rape and murder case and might need a lawyer, oh, and he didn't commit it"? They must hear protests of innocence all the time. He wanted to be careful about what he said, they might admit anything into court as evidence. After a few minutes he called back, this time leaving a message.

"My name is Omar Fassid. I'm calling to speak with Frank Jesperson. My father might need representation in what could end up being a high-profile case. Please call back to discuss."

Omar's hand shook as he hung up the phone. The wheels were set in motion. He only hoped true justice would prevail.

CHAPTER EIGHTEEN

The front door opened and Omar flinched. He didn't realize how used to living alone he'd become.

"I'm home." Brie paused in the entry to hang up her coat.

Omar smiled. He loved when she called the apartment home. Not just today, but every day. This felt so right. He rose from his chair and met Brie in the hall, suffocating her in an exuberant hug.

"Hey, honey, that's quite the greeting. Everything okay?"

Omar released her, but kept his hands on her shoulders.

"Been quite the tough day. Unbelievable actually. We need wine for this. You go change and I'll pour."

Brie caressed his cheek. "So sorry things have been difficult for you. I'll be quick." She gave his hand a squeeze and made her way down the hall to the bedroom.

Omar watched her go. *I'm so lucky.*

He rummaged through the cutlery drawer searching for the corkscrew. Everything had its place in his kitchen so he never had to look for anything. Brie, wasn't so particular. She opened the last bottle and hadn't put the corkscrew back in its place. He kneeled down to see the back of the drawer.

"Damn it!" A corn holder jammed into his thumb. Instinctively he stuck his thumb in his mouth and sucked. A disgusting reaction, but one his mother taught him to do as a child. "Keeps the dirt out," she used to say.

Brie strolled into the kitchen as he ran his thumb under cold water. "Oh no what happened?"

"It's nothing, just jammed a corn holder in my thumb searching for the corkscrew. Where is it?" His hands raised in exasperation.

Brie's face dropped. "Oh, sorry, I put it in the top drawer with the cutlery instead of the second drawer with the odds and ends. Guess I got out of the habit of ensuring I return things where you think they should go."

Brie opened the top drawer and reached to the back, pulling out the corkscrew.

Omar wrapped his thumb in a paper towel and retrieved a bottle of Cabernet Sauvignon from the wine rack at the end of the counter. He wanted to tell Brie it was okay, but it wasn't.

"I'll get it. Why don't you go find a band aid and then meet me in the living room? I'll throw a pizza in the oven too." She eyed him warily.

Omar stomped out of the kitchen. Such a little thing, but at the end of a day like today, it burrowed under his skin. At least the band aids were where they belonged. He glimpsed his reflection as he closed the cabinet door. After placing the band aid over the tip of his thumb, he ran his hand through his hair, massaging it back into place. Sunken eyes stared back at him. Today took a toll. He forced a smile and breathed deeply before turning off the light and strolling back down the hall. He needed to control his temper.

Brie sat on the edge of the couch, her head snapping to him as he entered the room.

God she's beautiful. He loved everything about her. Dark eyelashes framed cobalt eyes that seemed to see deep into his soul. But he especially like the look of that ring on her finger. He grabbed a wine glass off the table and snuggled in beside her. Sliding his hand over her thigh.

"Sorry, I'm grumpy." He tipped back the glass and took a large mouthful. The cherry notes filled his mouth and slid down his throat. He leaned back and closed his eyes.

A sigh escaped Brie's lips. "You've had a bad day. Tell me about it whenever you're ready." Brie slid her hand in his and stroked it, pressing down on the band aid that already lifted. She leaned forward and set her glass on the table, taking his thumb in both hands, readjusting the band aid and pressing it into place.

Omar opened one eye and peeked down as she placed his thumb on her lips and kissed it. He placed the wine glass on the table and leaned back. She straddled his hips and his hands rested on her back as she rubbed his temples.

"Now tell me, feeling any better?" She settled into his lap, rocking gently in place, keeping rhythm with her massage.

Omar grasped her hands and returned them to her sides, then lifted her up placing her beside him on the couch. He smiled and gave her a gentle kiss on the forehead.

"Brie there are some things I have to run by you." He paused taking another mouthful of wine. Brie leaned back into the soft leather of the couch with the wine glass in hand.

"Jahana visited Dad today without my knowledge."

Brie's eyes widened. "Is your dad okay? I'd think her showing up out of the blue wouldn't be good for him."

"He seems okay. I went to visit him. I couldn't wait to tell him about our engagement, but before I entered the room, I overheard them talking. Jahana offered to donate her kidney, on one condition."

Brie sat up. "That's fantastic Omar! Isn't this what you wanted?"

"The kidney, yes. The condition, no. She told him he has to plead guilty when he's charged in that cold case."

Brie set her glass on the table and reached for Omar's hand. "That's terrible. Did he agree to it?"

"Maybe? I left before the conversation ended because I didn't want them to catch me eavesdropping. Jahana makes me furious. I'm not sure if they said more after I left, but Dad agreed to the deal. I returned to talk to him later. He said she planned to donate a kidney, but didn't mention the deal. What does that mean?"

Brie remained silent, lost in thought. "There's one option here you know?"

"No there are two options: Dad can plead not guilty and die, or go to jail and live."

"There's one more. Maybe they won't ever charge him."

Omar took another swallow of wine. "Oh, I've thought about that, but it seems too good to be true. I'm sure they're just working on what they'll be charging him with. But, as each day passes, I have to admit hope grows a little stronger."

Brie crawled back in his lap. "So, I guess you didn't tell him about the engagement?"

"No, I'm afraid I'll have to hold off a little longer. Do you mind? Maybe take the ring off when you're around my parents until there's a good time to tell them?"

"You mean, sneak around? Pretend we're not engaged?" Her eyes sparkled as she settled into his lap.

The aroma of pizza filled the room, but they didn't notice.

****

Didar didn't expect to spend his retirement this way. Dialysis. What kind of life was this? He liked being out of the hospital, but the black cloud that followed him everywhere, drove him crazy.

One thing at a time. Deal with the kidney first, charges when they happen. He rubbed his temples. Pleading guilty would mean true misery.

Had Jahana told Omar about their deal? He suspected not. If she had, Omar would have said something. Jahana handed him his life on a silver platter, but, when he lifted the cloche, a severed head glared back; all his past deeds revealed in the clouds trapped within its eyes. Didar shuddered. When he closed his eyes, the image stared back at him and in the morning when he opened them, he thought of nothing else.

He'd never survive prison. Why get a transplant only to rot in jail? It'd be a waste of a kidney. There was a slim chance he wouldn't get charged. He could wait till something came up on the transplant list. Didar's phone interrupted his thoughts.

"Dad, we've got a surgery date. February 25. I'm calling Jahana to make sure she's heard. Dad, aren't you excited?" A long pause ensued. "Dad are you there? Everything okay?"

"Yes, I'm here. But I've been thinking about it and I don't think I can accept her kidney. Doesn't seem right for a parent to take a kidney from their child, no matter how old that child is. It doesn't leave her with a back-up. I wouldn't take one from you, so why should I take one from her?"

"But Dad there's no other option right now. And being a suspect in a rape/murder case there won't be one either. You might not like it, but you have to take it. There's no other choice." Desperation caught in Omar's voice.

Didar got it. He'd do anything to get Omar a kidney too. But Omar didn't understand the consequences of taking the kidney. Should he tell him? But if he was never charged, Omar would never have to find out. He didn't want to come between Omar and Jahana. And he didn't want them discussing the deal without him. And they would. Kids talking behind your back was just another injustice of old age.

"Why don't I give Jahana a call. No need for you to get in the middle of this. I need to be sure she wants to do this. It'll make me feel better about the surgery. What do you think?"

"Uh, yeah, I guess Dad if you want to. Do you think she'll mind if I pass on her number?"

Didar smiled. Omar didn't expect his old man to step up and talk to Jahana.

"No, can't imagine why she'd mind. She's giving me a kidney after all. Just text it to me."

Maybe he could talk Jahana out of making him plead guilty. But then he didn't want her to get cold feet and decide not to donate a kidney. He'd have to play this one very delicately. He wouldn't give up yet.

****

Jahana's daughters, Sahba and Cyra, stood side by side at the kitchen sink, rinsing dishes and loading the dishwasher. For once they weren't arguing. Their chatter, and peels of laughter told her they were getting along. Jahana moved to the living room not wanting to intrude. Things were more peaceful since Barid left. No doubt they felt the relief of their dad out of the house too. Life became easier. So far, he hadn't asked them to visit, although he called a couple of times to speak to them.

Her phone buzzed as she settled into the couch. The number wasn't familiar. But she recognized the area code; someone from New York. Something to do with the kidney transplant? She slid the arrow over and paused. "Hello?"

Before a voice there was a cough. Not a 'I've got something in my throat' cough. But a nervous cough. A tactic to delay talking. Jahana waited.

"Uh, hello. Is this Jahana?" Jahana immediately placed the voice.

"Yes, it is." Her words were abrupt.

"This is, uh, Didar."

Jahana's extremities suddenly became cold although she smiled at his uncomfortable reference to himself. At least he hadn't chosen 'father'. She might have hung up if he had.

"Yes, I recognized your voice." If he had the nerve to call, she wouldn't make this comfortable for him.

"Well, sorry to bother you. Just wondered if you know about the surgery date?"

Of course, she knew. She held the kidney.

"Yes, they called earlier today."

"Oh, good, good."

She waited for him to continue.

"One more thing, Jahana, are you sure you want to go through with this?"

It was not the question she expected. She thought he might try to convince her he shouldn't plead guilty. Now he made it sound like he cared about her.

"To tell you the truth, I've had lots of second thoughts after finding out this afternoon this surgery will take place so soon. How can I be sure you'll keep up your end of the deal if they don't charge you before surgery?"

"I thought you might be worried. And that's the real reason for my call. I have some questions. Why wouldn't you want this to go to trial where the truth will come out?"

"Because I know the truth. It's not a stretch for me to believe that if you raped my mother, you're capable of raping and murdering another. And the fact you won't admit to my mother's rape, tells me you likely wouldn't have trouble making up facts to suit yourself at a trial. A trial the family would be better off not having to sit through."

Another long silence followed. She refused to fill it.

"So, you haven't considered the possibility of justice? You want a guilty plea from a man who's not guilty? That's not justice. It gives the family false justice. In my sixty-nine years I've learned the grey area is much larger than the black and white."

Anger seeped into Jahana's voice. "Rape is rape. Murder is murder. There is no grey area."

"You're right. If they happened, there's no grey area. The grey area lies in interpreting the events. I only ask you to give me the opportunity to present my side of the story in a court of law if I'm charged. Allow the truth to come out."

Jahana rose from the couch, her knees shook. She sat back down. Why was it taking the police so long to sort this out when they had hard DNA evidence? And if they charged him, why didn't she want a trial? Did she have him all wrong? No, he needed to admit to his actions. The victim's family needed him to admit to what he'd done. She'd met charismatic men like him before. They could talk their way around anything. She wouldn't give him that opportunity.

"I'm sorry you're reneging on our deal. If you won't plead guilty once you're charged, I won't give you a kidney. It's as simple as that."

Didar sighed and guilt caused her stomach to turn. But she wouldn't negotiate her price for a kidney.

"Okay, but there's one more thing. I'm also sick about the fact you'll be giving up a piece of yourself for an old man like me."

The 'like me,' embedded itself in Jahana's psyche. A slip of the tongue? "So, why does an old man 'like you' think you don't deserve a kidney?"

"Oh, I just meant it seems wrong for offspring to be donating body parts to parents. Something ethically wrong is all. I meant an old man who shouldn't be taking organs from a… a daughter."

He'd said it. Called her a daughter. As much as she hated him, he called her a daughter. Somewhere deep inside, her resolve deepened. "I wouldn't worry about that aspect. If you were a complete stranger, I'd still save your life. In your case, I'm likely your only hope. And with that hope comes a deal. Are you going to keep your end of it? That's what this boils down to. It has nothing to do with how we're related and everything to do with whether you can keep your word."

"What kind of man takes his daughter's kidney though?"

Jahana straightened her shoulders. "What kind of man rapes and murders?"

156

He'd said what he thought she wanted to hear. He didn't have remorse over taking her kidney. Why would he? There was no remorse for what he'd done to her mother and the other victim of his urges.

"Okay Jahana, I relent. I'll keep my word. If you need anything, call me or Omar. I haven't told him about our deal and I'd appreciate it if you didn't either. It'll just cause a rift between you two. We'll be in touch. I appreciate what you're doing for me. Thank you."

"I'm going out on a limb here and trusting you to keep your end of the deal. I'm giving up one of my kidneys and I just ask you to have the decency to plead guilty and give that poor family closure. Do you really promise?

Didar coughed into the phone again before responding in a quiet, almost apologetic voice. "Yes, I promise."

"You damn well better."

Jahana touched the red circle without another word. She'd said enough and heard enough. And besides how do you end that conversation? Have a nice evening? Thanks for calling? You're welcome? Even goodbye seemed inappropriate.

Her knees shook as she strode into the kitchen.

"Who were you talking to Maman?"

"Oh, just someone I met recently. No one you know."

Both girls turned to her with a sparkle in their eyes.

"No, no. Not like that at all. Trust me girls, I've had enough of men for a while. This is something I need to talk to you about though. Come sit with me." Jahana sat at the island and patted the empty stools on either side.

"I found out I'm a match for someone who needs a kidney."

The girls stared at her with blank expressions.

"My DNA linked me to someone on MyGeneticFamily and he reached out to ask me if I would donate a kidney to his father if I'm a donor match. It turns out I am." Jahana patted the girls' knees.

"But Maman, what if you need that kidney? And what if you die in surgery?"

"No, no, it's a very safe surgery. Chances are I'll never need that second kidney, and he does. I can't very well say no, now can I?"

Both girls shook their heads.

"Girls, it'll be okay."

They didn't ask questions, so she brushed over the details.

CHAPTER NINETEEN

Didar lay on the stretcher outside the operating room in his curtained enclosure. Mahtob leaned over and kissed his cheek. Omar squeezed his hand when the porter announced he needed to wheel him through the doors which opened with the scan of his pass.

Didar clutched Mahtob's hand, not wanting to let go, but as the porter wheeled him through the open doors, her hand pulled away and he heard her gasp to choke back tears. Didar interlaced his fingers and rested his hands across his abdomen. He stared at the ceiling and pictured Omar reassuring Mahtob.

The fluorescent light flickered above as the stretcher's wheels tapped out a rhythm. He closed his eyes. It had been many years since he stepped inside a mosque, but he felt the need to pray. *Please watch over Jahana and help her heal. Help me keep up my end of this deal. Please help my body accept this kidney. Don't let Jahana's generosity go to waste. Please let this all work out. I promise I'll work harder to be a better person if it does.*

The stretcher stopped behind a curtain, and a nurse breezed in to attach a clip to his finger; all business, jaw clenched. He strove all his life to be the centre of the party, but this wasn't the party he'd had in mind.

"Can I get an extra blanket? Probably nerves, but I'm freezing."

Did she roll her eyes? He couldn't be sure, but she came back with a fresh blanket from the warmer. She snapped it open and unfolded it, no movements wasted.

"Better?" Her voice had a pleasant ring, but a sarcastic grin told him otherwise.

"Yeah, great, thanks."

She walked out of sight and Didar closed his eyes again. *How will this play out? The lawyer Omar contacted, Mr. Jesperson, seemed to think the delay in charging him was a good sign. Maybe they won't charge me at all. But if I'm charged and plead guilty, I'm guaranteed a life of unkindness, criticism, judgement, and confinement. Not just within the walls of a jail cell, but everywhere. Why am I getting this kidney?*

A voice pierced his thoughts. "Hello Didar, I'm Dr. Hadley."

Dr. Hadley explained the surgery. Didar tried to focus, but only heard the words he dreaded.

"Okay, are you ready?"

The nurse wheeled the stretcher into the operating room. He waited for the sterile environment to suffocate him, but the beautiful voice of Andrea Bocelli floated into the room punctuated with jokes and laughter of doctors and nurses. Did no one respect the fear he faced? He lay on his back helpless, counting back from one hundred.

CHAPTER TWENTY

Omar swallowed and sat up straight, hands clasped in his lap as he glanced from side to side, splitting the courtroom into the prosecution and the defence.

How did he get to this place? Just twenty-four hours ago, his dad went home following the kidney transplant. The police showed up two hours later.

"You're being charged with the first-degree murder of Laurie Dalton. You have the right…"

His dad remained stoic, like he'd been preparing for this all his life. He even smiled at them when they explained the charges.

"We took so long because we had to be sure the evidence was there to charge you with first degree as opposed to second degree murder, Mr. Fassid. There will be no charges of rape as the statute of limitations will not allow it."

In retrospect, Omar realized they'd been naïve hoping the police wouldn't pursue the case.

"We have the paperwork to take you into custody and to access medical files to ensure your needs are met while in custody. We'll try to get an arraignment hearing tomorrow morning. Bail will be discussed once you enter a plea."

Didar had turned to Omar as calmly as if he were preparing to leave on a business trip. "Son, call Mr. Jesperson and ask him to meet me at the police station."

Didar handed Omar his wallet and his watch.

"Stay here with your mom. Mr. Jesperson will call with the court details. I'll be fine. Don't come to the police station."

It was like the fight had gone out of Didar. Omar couldn't help but feel he'd keep his word and plead guilty. Would he ever come home again?

Omar put the wallet into his pocket and held the Rolex in his clenched fist, turning away from his dad. He ran his thumb over the crystal, cleared his throat, and turned back in time to see his dad shuffle towards the police officers who cuffed him and led him out the front door. Omar's body shook uncontrollably. Mahtob leaned on the door silent tears streaming down her face.

The wait for Mr. Jesperson's return call was excruciating. It was evening before they learned that arraignment would be the next day, right after lunch. Omar called Jahana to let her know. He wanted to ask about the deal with his dad, but he didn't know where to start. She was still in New York recovering from the surgery.

And so, seven days after a kidney transplant, he sat next to his mother in the front pew of a courtroom.

That morning the front-page headline read: Cold Case Solved: Murderer taken into custody. It was only a matter of time till they uncovered how Omar's DNA helped the police find the suspect.

Brie didn't come; Omar didn't want the media to tie her to them. She hadn't argued when he asked her to stay away from the trial. She seemed relieved not to be obligated to attend.

The defence table stood in front of him. He clasped his hands and bowed his head in an attempt to regain a sense of calm and stop shaking. The oak bench reminded him of church pews. *Fitting. Two places people go for redemption.*

Omar raised his head and turned to look at the victim's family. An elderly couple sat close together, a man and a woman about his dad's age on either side of them. They all stared straight ahead. The couple sat incredibly straight for the ages they must be. They were there before he arrived, so he had no idea which one used the cane that rested between them. He lowered his gaze. How difficult this must be for them, but this wasn't his dad's fault. He glanced up again and saw Jahana sitting in the row behind them. She wore her hijab pulled low. Their eyes met briefly before she looked away. Omar's stomach turned. In that moment he knew he'd heard the whole deal. His dad would plead guilty. He turned his attention forward and glanced at his mom.

Mahtob sat with her hands in her lap, back straight, face forward, unmoving; the poster child for dignity in the most undignified of circumstances. Taking his mother's lead, he too straightened. No one would interpret his actions as embarrassment. His dad was innocent, and a guilty plea wouldn't change his mind.

A hush fell over the courtroom, the tension palpable. The click of cameras and murmurs alerted Omar to the entrance of his father from the opposite side of the room, handcuffed, a bailiff at his side. Didar scanned the room for them. It seemed only yesterday Omar searched the crowd for his dad as he stood on stage at his grade three Christmas concert. Omar wanted to wave and comfort him, like Didar had done all those years ago. But he sat still, holding his breath. At last Didar's gaze rested on them, his shoulders relaxed and a smile entered his eyes. His mouth remained somber, caught between a smile and an apology; a face meant to reassure his mother before he sat with his back to them a few feet away. An innocent man with a burden of guilt. Omar reached across and covered his mother's hand with his. A quiver played at the corner of her mouth; tears trapped behind a stoic facade.

Omar forced himself to breathe. His insides rolled, nausea swept over him, unexpected. An abundance of saliva entered his mouth, and he swallowed several times to ward off the epigastric spasms likely to follow. He couldn't think about what his dad would do. *Tally something, anything.* Keeping his gaze straight ahead he counted the lines in the wainscoting surrounding the judge's bench. The spasms subsided; his breathing returned to normal.

"All rise. Judge Carrie Unger presiding."

Omar's breath caught. Mr. Jesperson said it would be Judge Kavanagh, a man known to run a fair and orderly courtroom. The defence lawyer turned and gave Omar a quick nod. He must have been informed of the change.

"You may be seated. Judge Kavanagh was called away for a personal emergency and I've been assigned this case in his absence. The purpose of the appearance today is to enter a plea and discuss bail. I don't anticipate this will take long." She paused for effect and stared at both the prosecution and defence before continuing. "We will begin with Mr. Didar Fassid's plea for the charge of murder in the first degree."

An audible murmur erupted. "Quiet, quiet. The gallery is full today. I ask you to be quiet. If you cause a disturbance to these proceedings, you will be removed from the courtroom."

The whispers subsided, and the courtroom fell into a deafening silence. Omar stared at his dad's back. He straightened a little more in his seat. This proceeding would not whittle away his dignity. Omar wished he could see Jahana's reaction, but she sat outside his periphery. Maybe he'd mistaken her body language. Maybe their deal didn't involve a guilty plea.

"… Mr. Didar Fassid, please rise."

Omar held his breath. Didar rose to his feet, confident in his slate blue Armani suit, hands no longer in cuffs clasped behind his back.

"Mr. Fassid, on the charge of first-degree murder, how plead you?"

His dad's knuckles turned white. Mahtob stared, unwavering. Omar reached for the railing in front of him and bent his head; a pose he regretted when it stared back at him from the front page the next day.

The pause elongated until the Judge repeated. "Mr. Fassid, how plead you?"

Didar cleared his throat. "Your honour, I plead…"

Time stood still in that fraction of a second. Didar's hands released their grip and fell to his sides, hanging as if they just let the last shred of hope escape. Omar closed his eyes and pictured his dad's face, smiling at him, he felt his dad's hand in his, he heard his laughter, heard his reprimands. Then he heard the words "not guilty." And the murmurs flowed through the gallery once again. The judge's gavel sounded, "Order, I said order!"

Omar turned to find Jahana. She glared back; a flash in her eyes said his dad reneged on the deal. The noise ceased as quickly as it erupted. Omar grabbed Mahtob's hand. She never had any reason to doubt his plea would be anything but not guilty.

Omar's elation grew tainted and, in that moment, he hated Jahana for making him question his dad's word.

Mr. Jesperson earned every dollar they paid him as he convinced the court to release his father on bail. The prosecution argued, but it was clear his father wasn't a flight risk and he needed care from his physician on a regular basis. Because of the seriousness of the charge, the judge added the contingent of an ankle monitoring bracelet as a condition of release on five hundred thousand dollars bail.

It was a concession they were willing to make.

The judge also advised an expedited trial due to his father's condition. Mr. Jesperson would receive disclosure of the evidence by the end of the week. The trial would begin in a month.

****

Jahana clenched and unclenched her fists. The hijab, fell to her shoulders, she no longer cared who noticed her. In fact, she wanted to be noticed. She'd be happy to talk to the press about the man she just donated a kidney to and tell them about how he broke his word. How he raped her mother. How his word wasn't worth seeking because lies flowed out of his mouth easier than air in an exhale. Her hands settled on her abdomen her right hand pressing on the scar. Part of her was missing and it lay inside this hideous man.

With shaking hands and knees wanting to buckle, she stood facing the front of the courtroom, staring into the back of Didar's head, willing him to turn and confront her. Face the lie he just committed.

But he didn't turn to look for her. He turned to his wife and Omar giving a reassuring smile. Bile rose in her throat.

How could she have been so stupid? She trusted him; gave him a kidney. Damn him. Why did she think he'd keep his word?

Tears of anger and humiliation stung her eyes. He wouldn't see her tears and misconstrue them for empathy or remorse. She cleared her throat, took a deep breath and stepped out into the aisle, joining the crowd exiting the courtroom. He wouldn't slide this by without addressing his lie. Everyone would know his true character by the time she finished with him.

Tears no longer threatened her composure, and she followed the throngs into the foyer situating herself behind the crowd outside the swinging courtroom doors. If she stood on her tip toes, she could see above the crowd. He had to come out soon. *What if he went out another door? What if he didn't have to come out this way?* Her heart quickened, but then the crowd parted and Omar, his mother, Didar and his lawyer stepped into the spotlight of cameras. She backed up to the wall and found her footing on a small ledge. From her new vantage point she glimpsed Didar's face. He glowed, enjoying the attention. *What kind of man enjoys this kind of attention? Is he a psychopath?* That thought had crossed her mind more than once.

She didn't hear the questions asked, or the answers given by the lawyer, but she saw their faces. All so pleased with themselves. They had it their way; a kidney and a trial.

She yelled above the noise. "And what about our deal, Didar? What happened with that?"

A startled expression crept over his face as he scanned the crowd for her. That look was almost worth the effort. The crowd turned, searching for the face behind the voice. She pulled the hijab up and bowed her head moving into the crowd. *He'd answer her question.*

Didar smiled when he spotted her at the front of the crowd. She paused, not expecting his smile and stepped back. Why wasn't he horrified about what she might say in front of the media? But his smile shone as charming as ever. Mahtob glanced from Didar to Jahana, confused, but retaining her composure in her perfectly coiffed hair, and navy skirt and jacket combo. Omar's eyes cast down while their lawyer continued to answer questions on behalf of the family.

Didar imperceptibly motioned for her to stand with them. Her eyes widened, and she stepped back waiting for the scrum to subside. The strength of support Mahtob and Omar displayed fascinated Jahana but she wouldn't be joining their camp.

Her feet tingled and pain shot through her arches. Why did she buy new shoes for this? He didn't deserve new shoes.

At last she heard the lawyer proclaim. "That's all the questions for now. Thank you."

And they were on the move. Jahana stepped in behind them and jostled to keep her place in close proximity. *He wouldn't get away before answering her questions.* And if Omar, Mahtob and the lawyer weren't aware of their deal, they'd find out.

The cold blast of air hit before she stepped out onto the steps of the courthouse. She lost sight of them and pushed a woman aside, sidestepping a reporter jostling for a better position. Then a hand grabbed hers. She pulled away and glanced up before realizing Omar held her hand. He led her down the stairs and into the waiting limousine. She covered her face with the hijab and slid into the limousine beside Omar, opposite Didar and Mahtob. Behind the tinted windows she let her hijab fall as her anger burst into the moment.

"How do you get to be free?" The words fell from her mouth, raw and cutting.

His face remained unemotional, then he lifted his pant leg to reveal a leg monitor as if that answered her question. Mahtob stared out the side window, ignoring her.

"That's not what I'm talking about and you know it, you fool."

Mahtob leaned forward, her words quiet but seething with anger. "Who do you think you are? Showing up now? Speaking to my husband that way? Omar offered you a safe haven from the mob out there and this is how you treat us?"

Jahana stiffened and sat back in her seat. How could she so vehemently protect this man? Mahtob's words may have caused her to pause, but it was a small pause where she recollected her thoughts and emotions.

"Didar, have you told Mahtob and Omar about our deal?"

Didar stared straight ahead; his expression unwavering.

"You remember the deal, don't you? The deal you went back on today? The one where I give you a kidney and you plead guilty? Surely you didn't forget I just gave you a kidney, and you didn't plead guilty?"

Mahtob stared at Jahana, mouth open. Was it horror or surprise etched on her face as she glanced from Jahana to Didar and back again? She searched their faces for an explanation.

Omar sat silently, eyes down studying the floor. He didn't appear angry or confused, just silent.

Jahana turned her anger to Omar. "You knew? How do you people live with yourselves?" She placed her hand on the door handle. The limo slowed to a stop. The mob outside was preferable to this close-knit group of liars.

Didar leaned forward and placed his hand on hers. "Jahana wait. I can explain."

She paused and took her hand off the door handle, recoiling at his touch. "Really? You can explain why you made a deal with me, knowing all along you were going to screw me? I guess it's no different from how you screwed my mother and that innocent person you also murdered?"

Mahtob raised her hand, but Didar grabbed it and held it firmly.

"I don't blame you for being angry. I intended to plead guilty and keep my end of the bargain, I truly did. But when I sat down in that courtroom today and heard the judge ask for my plea, I had to be honest. I'm not guilty and could not, under oath, say I was."

Jahana slumped back, deflated. She raised her head and looked Didar in the eye. "Then why did you agree to our deal?"

"You said you wanted the victim's family to get closure. Me too. I realize me admitting to a crime I didn't commit might give them closure, but it would be a false sense of closure. Their true closure will come through a trial. If you believe I'm guilty, then let the justice system prove it."

Jahana opened and closed her mouth, unable to form an intelligent response. As much as she hated to admit it, she understood his side of the argument. *What if he wasn't guilty? But the DNA proved it.*

Omar's voice sounded small and distant. "You have every reason to distrust our father."

Mahtob winced and turned to stare out the side window again.

"But unlike you, I've known him all my life and I can say without hesitation that if our dad says he's not guilty, he's not guilty. I get why you need to see proof of that. Isn't that what a trial is for? To prove guilt?" His voice trailed off.

"Let me out." She tried the door handle, but the door remained locked. "Let me out!"

Didar leaned back and mumbled through the screen to the driver before turning back to Jahana. "We'll let you out around the corner. There's a hotel nearby with taxis. That way you can avoid the mob."

Jahana stared at Didar, incredulous. He owed her his life. He'd pay for his past. She tried the door again as the car rolled to a stop in front of the hotel. It popped open, and she stepped out, slamming it behind her without looking back.

CHAPTER TWENTY-ONE

Omar knew what a spanking was, but that awareness never made them any easier to face. He stood in the garage, knees shaking. He'd never been spanked in the garage before. Didar removed the belt from his pants, folded it in two and snapped it with a flick of his wrists. The crack made Omar jump. He stared at the floor, spotless. Not an oil stain or grease mark, tiles wiped to a shine. His reflection stared back as he focused on his feet.

Omar waited silently. His dad stood before him. The silence stretched on longer than he ever remembered it stretching on before.

Omar wondered when his dad would decide he was too old for spankings. His thirteenth birthday had just passed. When would his dad resort to another form of punishment? He wasn't a bad kid. No smoking or drinking like most of his friends. All he did was skip school to hang out at a friend's house for the afternoon. They played video games and ate Cheetos.

"Do you enjoy hurting me?" Didar snapped the belt another time for effect. Omar kicked at the floor, continuing to cast his eyes down.

"I asked a question. Answer me, Son." His dad's voice boomed.

Was he in the garage so his mom couldn't interfere if the beating got out of control?

Omar raised his eyes and met his dad's gaze with remorse. "No, I don't enjoy hurting you. It had nothing to do with you." He winced. He knew better than to embellish; just answer the question.

"Nothing to do with me! When the school calls to tell me you skipped school, it has everything to do with me."

Yep, shouldn't have brought up the 'nothing to do with you' bit. Omar's eyes dropped back to the floor. *Just get it over with already.*

"Look at me."

Omar raised his head and stared blankly; his jaw clenched.

"If you want to hurt me, do it now." Didar offered the belt to Omar. "Go ahead take it. Here's your chance to take it out on me. Go ahead. Hit me."

Omar's jaw dropped. His hands remained stuffed in his pant pockets.

"Take it. Come on. This is the opportunity you've been waiting for your whole life. Trust me, you can't hurt me as much with this belt as you can by your behaviour. Lying and sneaking around. That's hurtful. This belt..." Didar paused and his eyes filled with tears. He cleared his throat and continued. "This belt can't hurt me. But your actions can and they have. Be careful what you say and do, Son. Remember no matter how much this belt has hurt you in the past, it's nothing compared to how much you can hurt the ones you love with careless, selfish actions. Now, here, take it."

Didar grabbed Omar's arm and forced open his palm, wrapping his fingers around the belt. Omar swallowed and stared at the belt. A few minutes earlier he might have used it, but now his fist opened and the belt fell to the floor, his eyes resting on it. He raised his head and met his dad's gaze, silent tears streaming down his face. He turned and walked out of the garage.

He should have apologized, but no apology could rectify the way he'd made his dad feel.

CHAPTER TWENTY-TWO

The limousine door closed, and the driver pulled away from the curb. Didar raised his hand before Mahtob said anything.

"Listen, I didn't tell you about the deal because it would've upset you. And I didn't plead guilty, so if Jahana hadn't unleashed her fury, you wouldn't have even known of that side of the story to this nightmare." He rubbed his pulsing temples.

"Are you okay, Dad?" Omar glanced at his mom, then his stare rested on Didar.

"Yeah, I'm fine. Just can't wait to get home and lie down."

"But you should have told me. I'm on your side. I'm here to be your cushion, your support. We don't hide things from each other, remember?" Mahtob's eyes pled with him. He nodded. He should have told her.

"I didn't want you to talk me out of keeping my word. I planned to plead guilty, but the other day on the news the family of a murder victim expressed how a guilty plea took away their opportunity to understand the case. They felt there might be other victims out there that could benefit from a full scrutiny of the case. That's when I questioned my plea. If I pled guilty, they would never find the real murderer."

"So, you knew before today you wouldn't plead guilty?"

"No, I walked into that courtroom prepared to lodge a guilty plea. But something about being there and swearing an oath to tell the truth brought that newscast back and swayed me to plead not guilty."

"And you don't think I had a right to know what you were thinking? You don't think your plea wouldn't affect me?"

Didar clasped his wife's hands. "It affects you. I felt caught between a rock and a hard place. How do I renege on a deal with someone who just saved my life? This looks bad. If I can't keep my word with Jahana, how can I be trusted?"

"If you can't share your deepest darkest secrets with your wife, how can you be trusted?" Mahtob pulled her hands away and stared out the side window. Then turned her attention to Omar. "And you knew? Didar, did you tell him and not me?"

"No, Mom, I overheard Jahana talking to Dad the day she came to the hospital. He never said a word about it. Neither did Jahana. So, I kept my mouth shut, hoping they altered the deal after I stopped eavesdropping."

"Okay, can we stop all of this! No more secrets. No more pretending. I promise. Let's all three of us vow to tell each other everything. It's the only way we'll get through this." Didar's face flushed.

Omar and Mahtob glanced at each other and nodded.

"You're right Dad. We need to support and protect each other. We aren't doing ourselves any favours by keeping secrets."

The red from Didar's face melted away.

As the limo turned onto their street, the crowd made it clear they would have to stick together. They set media trucks up on both sides of the street. People milled about on the lawn.

"Okay Dad, here's what will happen. I'll jump out first, followed by you, then Mom. Stick close and don't stop to talk to anyone. Give me your keys. Once we're inside, I'll call the police and have them do some crowd control. These people are trespassing."

Didar sighed; his stomach turned. He did as he was told.

****

"I don't recall."

The words echoed and caused a murmur to cascade over the courtroom.

Omar's stomach turned. Mr. Jesperson tried to dissuade Didar from testifying, but he insisted. He claimed he wanted the victim's family to hear from him so they would know he wasn't responsible for her death.

Didar listened when Mr. Jesperson drilled Didar, preparing him for his turn on the stand. So, his dad's response didn't surprise him. He glanced at the jury. Did his dad's inability to recall the night, or the woman, hurt his case? A few jurors scowled. Omar returned his gaze to his father on the stand.

"So, you don't recall where you were on the night of May 9, 1981 at 11:00 pm?"

"No, I don't recall." Didar's face remained unemotional. He answered questions without embellishing, just like they practiced.

"Do you recall where you were earlier that night?"

"No, that was 38 years ago. I do not recall."

"Do you recognize this woman?" The prosecution presented a picture to Didar. He studied it.

"I do not." The prosecutor returned to her table and picked up a stack of papers. She laid them on the witness stand.

"We have witnesses who have testified Laurie Dalton left the Thirsty Duck at 11:00 pm the evening before with a man that matches your description. Did you often leave bars with women back then?"

Mr. Jesperson jumped to his feet. "Objection your honour. What does whether he left bars with women on other days have anything to do with this case?"

The prosecution countered. "It helps establish the character of Didar Fassid, your honour."

"I'll allow. Answer the question Mr. Fassid."

"Yes, I did often leave bars with women in those days."

Omar turned his attention back to the jury. They kept their emotions in check for the most part, but one woman sat with her head cocked to one side and stared at Didar with disdain in her eyes. She might be a problem.

He glanced at his mother. Her expression remained stoic. She stared straight ahead at Didar. Unwavering.

"Would you consider yourself to have been a womanizer back in 1981?"

Mr. Jesperson jumped to his feet again. "Objection your honour. Irrelevant."

"Sustained."

"Okay, I'll put it another way. Did you have respect for women in 1981?"

Omar held his breath.

Didar paused before answering. "I was young and didn't respect women the way I do now. But I always respected a woman's right to say no."

Omar strained his neck to see Jahana sitting on the prosecution's side of the room. She returned his stare, eyes wide. Omar directed his attention back to the front of the room.

"Is that so, Mr. Fassid?" The prosecutor paused and looked at the floor as if she was debating her next question. Her head snapped up and she stepped toward Didar. "Is it true you have a daughter who is the product of a sexual assault?"

The courtroom erupted.

"Order, I said order." The gavel hit the judge's bench, and the courtroom quieted.

Mr. Jesperson leaped to his feet. "Objection your honour. These facts are not in evidence and are hearsay."

Journalists' cameras flashed as if they could capture words. This would be something they grabbed onto just like they did when they realized it was Omar's posting on GENmatch which helped the police tracked down his father. The media surrounded his apartment building and his mom and dad's house. They made the evening news every day.

Omar turned to Jahana again. This time she looked away.

Mr. Jesperson continued. "Mr. Fassid is not on trial for sexual assault. I object to this line of questioning and ask that the prosecutor's question be omitted from the record."

"Sustained. Ms. Scarlet please keep your questions to the charge of murder in the first degree. The jury is to disregard the question presented by Ms. Scarlet.

Omar breathed a sigh of relief. He glared at Jahana. How could she talk to the prosecution about their father?

"Okay, Mr. Fassid. They found your DNA on Laurie Dalton's underwear, on the murder weapon and on a cigarette butt recovered at the scene. How do you explain this?"

Omar noticed Didar's gaze wavered. He glanced at Mahtob, but then regained his composure and looked the prosecutor in the eye. "It's clear I had intercourse with this woman. And I must have smoked a cigarette. At some point I must have also touched the brick."

"But you don't recall?"

"No, I do not."

"I'm about to show you photos of the victim's body. Let me explain what you'll see. Bruises covered Ms. Dalton's body. Tears were evident in her genital area. Blood covered her head from an injury sustained by the brick with your DNA on it. Even though a lot of blood was evident on the outside of her head, they have established an intracerebral bleed caused her death. I want you to look closely Mr. Fassid and tell me again whether you recognize her."

The prosecution walked over to Didar and placed three large photos on the witness stand. Omar watched his dad stare at the photos. No emotion showed on his face. No horror, no remorse, nothing. Then his voice pierced the courtroom.

"I don't recognize her. As for the tearing and bruising, that does sometimes happen during rough sex. Consensual rough sex. I do not deny I may have had sex with this woman, but I did not rape her. And would never have killed her."

"Would it be part of rough sex to smash a brick into the side of her head?"

"No, it would not."

"You say you didn't hit her with the brick? But you also say you can't remember anything from that night." Omar searched the faces of the jury. Another woman sat forward, her eyes blazing. They were losing the jury one person at a time.

"I know, because I could never kill anyone. Regardless of how much I had to drink."

Three of the jurors stared at the floor.

"Where did you wake up the next morning?"

"No idea. Again, it was 38 years ago. I likely went home to my apartment."

"Did you live with anyone at that time?"

"No, I did not."

"Did you keep a journal or a day planner?"

"No."

"The day after the event, was a Sunday. What was your usual routine on Sundays at that time?"

"If I had been out drinking the night before I would likely have stayed in bed till early afternoon. I might have met up with friends later in the day, or gone for a run if I was feeling up to it. Sundays were days I recovered from the night before and got ready for the work week."

"So, you didn't have any regular routines on Sunday. Going to Mosque? Dinner with family or friends?"

"No, I did not."

"No more questions your honour."

Mr. Jesperson rose, slowly striding toward the witness stand.

"Didar, you're aware there was a cigarette at the scene with your DNA on it, correct?"

"Yes."

Mr. Jesperson turned toward the jury and asked his next question. "Do you have a cigarette after sex?"

Didar cleared his throat and bowed his head. "In those days, yes. I no longer smoke."

"If you had hit this woman with a brick, would you have stayed around to have a cigarette?"

"I wouldn't have hit her. The only way I would have had a cigarette, though, is if we had both enjoyed the sex and we stayed around after to enjoy a smoke."

"Even if the sex was in an alleyway?"

"Yes. From what I understand, there was an empty bottle of tequila at the scene. I don't drink tequila, but I could imagine sticking around and having a cigarette while she had a drink."

"You are correct. The bottle at the scene only had the victim's DNA on it. Thank you, Didar. No more questions your honour." Mr. Jesperson returned to his seat and leafed through some papers on the table.

Omar eyed the jury. Which way did they sway? The prosecution had already presented expert witnesses that corroborated the DNA evidence and the way the brick struck the victim's head. They painted a damning picture for his dad: at the scene, DNA on the murder weapon, he had sex with the victim and smoked a cigarette or at least finished smoking a cigarette while there.

But the fact he had no recollection of the events, how could he defend himself? It came down to whether his dad struck her with a brick.

The bruising and what appeared to be forced entry didn't help either. But he explained, as embarrassing as it was for Omar to hear, that he liked his sex rough and sought partners that did too. Omar didn't want to think about what that meant regarding his relationship with his mom.

The prosecutor rose. "I have one more question your honour." She turned her attention to the witness stand.

"Mr. Fassid, is it possible you smoked the cigarette before you had sex? Perhaps you left the bar and lit up a cigarette while walking with Laurie Dalton?"

"I suppose that's a possibility, yes."

"Thank you. Your honour the prosecution has no further questions."

The defence only had one more witness.

Mr. Jesperson rose. "Your honour I call Dr. Maxwell to the stand as an expert witness in crime scene re-enactment."

Omar sat up straight. Their hopes all hinged on this man's testimony.

"Dr. Maxwell, the prosecution explained to the jury the victim's head was hit with a brick found at the scene. Are there any other possibilities that might account for the intracerebral hemorrhage that killed Laurie Dalton?"

"Yes, she may have fallen and hit her head on the brick."

"Can you please explain how that could happen?"

Omar watched Dr. Maxwell as he explained with diagrams how Laurie Dalton may have fallen in her inebriated state and hit her head. She may not have knocked herself out and rolled into the position they found her. Omar caught himself holding his breath. He exhaled.

The prosecution took their turn trying to discredit his forensic abilities. And it wasn't hard. He had been proven incorrect in his assumptions in other court cases, but the prosecution didn't prove him incorrect in this case. Omar hoped that stuck with the jury.

Day six of the trial ended. Closing statements would wrap it up in the morning.

****

Jahana glanced across the courtroom. Omar and his mother sat in the front row of the gallery, behind Didar. As much as she detested them all, she had to admire their loyalty. She shook her head. How could they stand behind this monster who murdered a woman after raping her? It didn't matter what he'd done since, it would never be enough to garner forgiveness.

"I ask you to consider the facts in the case." The prosecutor paced the floor in front of the juror's box.

"A man matching Didar Fassid's description left the Thirsty Duck on May 9, 1981 at 11:00 pm with Laurie Dalton. Both appeared intoxicated. Early the next morning Ms. Dalton's body was found, bruised, sexually assaulted and the murder weapon, a brick, lay close by. A brick with Mr. Fassid's DNA on it. We heard testimony from our forensics team the brick was used to hit her on the head. She suffered a brain bleed and died shortly after. Mr. Fassid's DNA was found at the scene in two additional places; on Ms. Dalton's underwear and on a cigarette butt."

The prosecutor stopped pacing and faced the jury, placing both hands on the rail.

"The DNA evidence all points to Mr. Fassid brutally raping and murdering Ms. Dalton. By his own admission, he likes his sex rough. Add alcohol to the mix and it's clear, he crossed the line. He claims to remember nothing of the night, or has he just spent the last 38 years trying to forget it? Mr. Fassid's behaviour at the time was reckless, so reckless he committed murder by hitting Ms. Dalton over the head with a brick. His DNA on the brick places it in his hand. In fact, it's plain he picked it up and savagely attached Ms. Dalton. Smashing her skull, causing her death."

The prosecutor paced again.

"His theory that he sat with her after enjoying a cigarette while she drank is preposterous. Any woman with the bruises and tears she experienced, would not be sitting on hard pavement enjoying a drink with the man who just assaulted her. You saw the images. Mr. Fassid's story just doesn't line up.

She paused and turned to Didar, pointing her finger. "But what lines up is the evidence." She turned back to the jury and continued. "And I ask you to think about that in your deliberations. While you can't convict him of rape due to the statute of limitations on that crime, you can convict him of the second crime he committed that night, first degree murder."

She pointed again towards the defence table. "The defence talked about how Mr. Fassid has led a good life, been an upstanding citizen, a well-known businessman. Don't be swayed by what he appears to be. Consider the facts. He's a monster who has kept a secret for 38 years and has refused to admit the role he played in the death of an innocent woman."

The prosecutor slowly turned and strode back to her table, her black pumps creating exclamation points on the marble floor with each step. She sat down with deliberate care, regaining eye contact with each juror.

Mr. Jesperson rose and approached the jury. His Oxfords silent on the same marble floor. He turned and pointed at the prosecutor.

"Ms. Scarlet would have you believe there is no reasonable doubt in this case." He leaned in, both hands gripped the jury box railing.

"But I think you've all heard there is more than reasonable doubt. What I think we can all agree on is Mr. Fassid and Ms. Dalton had sex on the night of May 9, 1981. We can agree Ms. Dalton passed away sometime after they had sex, sex which by Mr. Fassid's own admission and by the evidence shows was rough. They had both been drinking and Mr. Fassid had smoked a cigarette. Somehow Ms. Dalton succumbed to an injury invoked by a brick found at the scene. I think we can all agree on those facts."

Jahana noticed slight nods from a few jurors. The rest remained quiet, unemotional. Mr. Jesperson turned toward the prosecution and raised his voice.

"What the prosecution has not proven is that Didar Fassid hit Ms. Dalton on the side of her head with a brick." He whirled around and faced the jury. "And that is the crux of this case. Has the prosecution proven beyond a reasonable doubt that Mr. Fassid hit Ms. Dalton with the brick? No, they have not. The brick had traces of his DNA on it, but it doesn't mean he hit her with it. Perhaps he moved it out of their way. Perhaps he tripped on it and picked it up and threw it to the side. And perhaps Ms. Dalton, in a very inebriated state as evidenced by her blood alcohol levels tested on the intracranial clot, fell and hit her head on the brick and then crawled a short distance before becoming unconscious."

Mr. Jesperson paused and scanned the jury. Jahana noticed a few of them looked down, not meeting his gaze. She swallowed the lump growing at the back of her throat.

"This is a sad case. An innocent life lost 38 years ago. But with the evidence at hand, there's still reasonable doubt because the circumstances can be explained another way. Mr. Fassid has a wife of 35 years and a grown son who have sat behind the defence table every single day of this trial. If he were not a good man, a man incapable of murder, do you think they would be here publicly supporting him? Do you think he could have built a successful business? Do you think he would have the standing in this community that he has built?"

Mr. Jesperson paused again and backed away from the jurors, raising his hands and dropping them to his sides. "In fact, I'm surprised that a case with so many explanations for the evidence presented, even made it to court."

More jurors avoided the defence attorney's eye.

"Don't get me wrong, I'm empathetic to this family who have sought closure for their daughter's death. But sometimes there is no one to blame. Sometimes death is an accident as it was in Laurie Dalton's case."

Mr. Jesperson stood gazing at the jurors then returned to his seat.

He'd made a point, but the prosecution said upfront he would try to sway the facts. Surely, they'd see through his tactics.

Once the jury left for deliberations, Jahana rose and walked out of the courtroom alone. So far, the press hadn't figured out she was the product of the sexual assault. She hadn't worn the hijab since that first day and so far, the media hadn't identified her as the daughter conceived by rape. So far, she'd remained anonymous. She exhaled slowly as she pushed through the courtroom door into the hallway.

****

"Jahana, Jahana!" Omar ran after her as she left the courtroom. He noticed reporters watching him and trying to figure out who Jahana was. That was when he realized he blew her cover. They'd be searching for the daughter who had sided with the prosecution. He felt a twinge of guilt for giving away the fact she was sitting in the courtroom, but she was trying to sink their father's case. And he was happy it backfired.

She glanced back once, but pushed forward with renewed determination to get away from the reporters and perhaps him too.

He lost sight of her as reporters came between them. He grabbed people and pulled himself forward making his way out the front doors of the courthouse. Cold winds stirred the dusting of snow into a frenzy. He spotted Jahana getting into a taxi. He sprinted down the steps and pounded on the taxi door just before it pulled away. The driver braked and dipped his head and gestured to Jahana. "I'm taken."

Omar searched Jahana's face. "Come on Jahana, I just want to talk to you." She rolled her eyes but opened the door and scooted over to the other side.

Omar slid into the seat and pulled the door behind him. Photographers gathered outside; flashes bounced off the windows.

"Drive," Omar ordered, "Get us out of here."

The taxi pulled away. "Where am I headed? Omar had no idea what hotel she stayed at.

"The Hilton, Manhattan East." She glared at Omar. "I suppose you're here to tell me what a shitty thing I did by talking to the prosecution?"

Omar paused before replying. "I can't believe you'd do that. This case is about a murder, not a sexual assault. And the prosecution knew their question wouldn't be admissible. They just wanted to garner support by bringing in irrelevant hearsay. It was a cheap trick. But that's not what I need to talk to you about."

Jahana's face flushed and her fingers interlaced, knuckles white. "It's not irrelevant to me. But anyway, why are you here then."

"I've said this before, but you don't know our father like I do."

"Oh, did you know he likes 'rough' sex?" Jahana interrupted, eyes searching his soul.

"Uh, no, not till yesterday. That still doesn't make him a rapist or murderer. His sex life is his business, and it's humiliating to drag it through the court."

"Do you hear yourself? It's not pictures of your dad's body naked and abused being passed around the court. And then insinuations that she asked for it. She liked it rough? Really?"

"She must have. My dad wouldn't hurt anyone. Perhaps the sex got out of hand because of the drinking, but he would never have murdered her."

"Is that what you think happened with my mom too? Sex that got out of hand? An attack on a Jewish girl, by a man of power?"

Silence filled the cab. "Jahana, I can't say for certain what happened with your mother. My dad has lots of regrets and he's lived his life trying to make up for them. He's not a monster. He's not a threat to anyone. But most of all he's not a murderer. I hope I can help you see that."

Jahana stared at her feet, the tears in her voice unmistakable, "You will never help me see he's not a monster. I'm alive because he's a monster. I feel so much guilt about that. Guilt that he should own, not me. But he doesn't own any of it, so I have to."

The taxi pulled in front of the Hilton. Jahana reached into her purse and pulled out a crumpled twenty and handed it to the driver. She got out of the cab without another word.

What was left to say?

"Now where?" The cabby's voice penetrated his thoughts.

"Back to the courthouse." *Damn.*

He pulled out his phone. Messages filled his screen. He hadn't told his mom he'd left the courthouse and now, the two of them were holed up in a backroom waiting for him to come get them. He texted her back.

Sorry, on my way. Be there in 15 minutes.

The phone slid off his knee to the seat. Omar leaned back on the headrest. He visualized the tears he wished he could let escape, sliding down his throat, a trick he learned as a kid. Somehow it helped. He called it his silent cry.

****

"Where were you, Son? We were worried?" Didar rose as Omar entered the room. They'd been waiting for him for more than a half hour.

"Sorry. I caught up with Jahana. I wanted to have a talk with her."

Didar glanced at Mahtob. "Do you think that's a good idea?" They walked down the hall in relative peace, the reporters gone for the day.

"No, but I wanted to talk to her about her discussion with the prosecution and the dirty pool they're playing."

Didar shook his head. "Oh Omar, she's caught in this thing. She doesn't understand. If I was in her shoes, I'd likely have done the same thing. Don't get angry with her over it."

Mahtob's eyes flashed at Didar. "Don't get angry with her? Are you kidding? She's trying to take you down. What kind of daughter does that?"

Didar cleared his throat. "A daughter that doesn't know her father and whose mother has her convinced I raped her. There's nothing we can do about that right now. Let's just focus on the trial. The judge didn't allow the question, so it's a moot point."

Mahtob shook her head. "She has you all wrong."

"The press knows who she is now. I chased her down the hall calling her name."

"Oh Omar, why did you have to do that?"

"I didn't mean to, I just did it trying to get her attention. With the reporters watching me I realized I gave her to them. I feel badly about that, but what did she expect when she decided to help the prosecution? They'd have found her, eventually."

"You're probably right, but I wish, for her sake she stayed anonymous."

The limo waited for them and a few reporters loitered, hoping to get some kind of response. Omar ran interference and he and Mahtob crawled into the car. Omar pushed his way to the other side and got in without too much trouble.

"So, Dad we need to talk about a Plan B."

"What do you mean?" Didar rubbed his temples. He just wanted to leave it in the courtroom. Nothing more could be done now.

"We need to prepare for whatever the verdict the jury comes back with."

"It will come back as not guilty. No need to think otherwise." Didar tilted his head towards Mahtob. This conversation could wait.

Omar ignored him and continued. "That's what we're hoping for, but what if it comes back guilty? We'll appeal, right?"

Didar glared at Omar and tried to level his voice. "Like I said, we won't have to worry about that."

"But how do you know?"

"Because I'm not guilty, that's how I know." Didar raised his voice. "Enough of this talk. I just want to go home, have a bath and early dinner so I can go to bed. I'm exhausted."

"But…"

"I said enough. No more."

Mahtob shook and tears streaked down her cheeks.

"Now see what you've done to your mother?"

Mahtob dabbed at her eyes. "It's okay, I just don't want to think of anything except a not guilty verdict, but Omar is probably right. We should talk about it."

"Not today."

Didar watched Omar and Mahtob acquiesce. He still had control in this family and they'd bloody well listen to him.

The limo rolled up to the house and Omar opened his door first to make a path through the reporters to the house. Didar hoped the extra attention from reporters would end soon. People would forget and his life would return to normal. The retired life he planned. Coffee with the men at the neighbourhood coffee shop on most mornings. Dropping in to the business to see how things were going. Broadway plays with Mahtob.

He let out a sigh. That would be his life. He wouldn't see it any other way.

****

Jahana watched herself run from the courthouse as CNN replayed the footage on an incessant loop. It had been two days, and they were hungry for information. They hadn't found her yet. She remained in her hotel room despite the lousy room service. It beat the alternative of being recognized.

Her phone buzzed to life, and she jumped. The prosecutor promised to contact her when the jury reconvened. They were being called to the courthouse.

Jahana tucked in her hijab, bringing it forward more than she normally would. Guilt rose as she did so. She used the hijab to hide, not for its intended religious purpose. She grabbed her purse and caught a cab outside the lobby. The driver glanced at her in the mirror, his eyes narrowing and then, they lit up with recognition.

"Hey aren't you the woman the reporters are all lookin' for? The daughter of that guy up on murder charges?"

Jahana gave him a piercing glance before peering out the side window.

"Makes no difference to me. Glad you're standing up to that bastard. I hope he goes away for life."

Jahana continued to stare out the window, avoiding his persistent glances.

She arrived before the crowd, although the reporters gathered. She hopped out of the cab and kept her head down.

"Hey it's her!"

She quickened her pace making it into the courthouse before they caught up with her. Then someone grabbed her elbow and steered her into a side hallway. She adjusted her hijab and peered up at the prosecutor.

"I'm sorry you got caught up in this."

Jahana smiled weakly, happy for the diversion away from the reporters, but something Omar said stuck with her. "Hey, I have a question. Did you know your question wouldn't be admissible?"

The prosecutor didn't have to answer, her face said it all.

"You did it just to sway the jury?"

"Listen, sometimes you have to do little things to get an edge."

"Little? Do you call what I did little? And now the press will be all over me. You're no better than the defence spinning half-truths. I don't appreciate being used."

They reached the side entrance to the courtroom. Jahana held back.

"I'm sorry you feel that way. Trust me, my question made an impression with the jury even if they can't consider it. Coming forward to me helped the case."

Jahana motioned for her to go ahead. She hated being used. She'd face the throng and enter the courtroom where the public entered. Besides, she needed a bathroom.

Just inside the foyer to the courtroom, Jahana ducked into the public washroom. She halted halfway into the room. Mahtob stood at the sink, frozen at Jahana's reflection in the mirror.

Should she leave? Turn around right now and walk out the door? No, I'm not the one on trial here. She stepped inside and let the door close behind her.

Mahtob turned the faucet handle and busied herself with tucking hair behind her ear and checking her eye makeup.

"Hey, look…"

Mahtob spun to face her and raised her hand. Jahana stopped mid-sentence.

"I don't want to talk to you. I'm sorry you have gone through so much, but you don't know my husband. He's not the man you think he is."

Jahana clenched her fists, swallowing the bile rising in her throat. She took a deep breath before speaking, sarcasm dripping from her tone. "Why don't you tell me what a good husband he is then?" She turned to the stalls, noting they were all empty. She had no desire to hear how wonderful Didar was. But somehow Mahtob missed the sarcasm and continued.

"He has always treated me right and has been a wonderful father. Before we married, he told me he had some regrets in life. I know about the women he slept with and that he… he liked sex a certain way. He's never been unfaithful to me. He's a good man."

Jahana whirled around. "How do you explain my existence then? My mother's rape and pregnancy?"

"I think perhaps your mother couldn't admit she had consensual casual sex. She became pregnant and had to explain it somehow."

Heat crept up Jahana's neck and beads of sweat formed at her temples. "How dare you! Is that what Didar told you? Can you even think for yourself? Two separate claims of rape and you take his word for it and dismiss it?"

Mahtob stared back at Jahana. "If you knew him, you would understand how he could never do what you're claiming. I'm sorry you didn't grow up around him. If you had you'd understand."

Mahtob picked up her purse and strode to the door. She paused and extended an olive branch. "I'm sorry for your pain." And then she opened the door and stepped out into the mob. Jahana entered the stall and let the door slam. Tears stung her eyes. *My pain? What about the victim's pain? My mother's pain? The jury will see right through him.*

She waited until the din outside the bathroom died down then crossed the foyer, staring straight ahead and walking down the aisle in the courtroom. Eyes watched her and a few people offered her a seat, but she kept moving straight to the front of the room. The actions of her father would not shame her. She squeezed into the bench behind the victim's family and kept her gaze on the front of the room.

****

"All rise..."

Mahtob stared ahead, glancing at Omar and patting his hand. He searched her face. Without turning up the corners of her mouth, she smiled. A calm about her exuded more determination than he'd ever seen. Maybe she agreed with Didar's not-guilty belief. Or with the decision that lay in the hands of the jury. Whatever calm she found in that restroom, he needed it now.

His knees shook as he rose. He studied the back of his dad who stood straight with all the confidence Omar felt slipping away. He studied the jurors as they filed in. None of them so much as glanced at Didar. They appeared tired and frazzled. Murmurs grew behind him as the crowded courtroom discussed their speculations.

"Order." The gavel came down twice. The murmurs ceased. Omar held his breath.

"Please be seated. The jury has deliberated for two days and from what I understand, they would like some clarification on the instructions provided to them at the end of the trial. There has been no decision made in the way of a verdict."

Didar bowed his head; relieved or worried?

The judge continued. "I have received the following question from the jury: Can you please provide clarification regarding reasonable doubt? Jurors have different interpretations."

The women jurors and two of the men averted their eyes downward. The remainder stared at the judge.

Mahtob grabbed Omar's hand, leaning close. "Reasonable doubt, that's a good sign... isn't it?"

Omar shrugged and shook his head. What should he make of it? The words 'hung jury' echoed in his head. One person needed to change their mind either way. The judge's response to their query could make a huge difference in the outcome.

The judge turned to the jury. "Thank you for your diligence in deliberations. In regard to your request I will repeat the instructions presented to the jury explaining reasonable doubt." Judge Unger's attention did not waiver from the jury. Her words were slow and clear. She removed her glasses and waived them at the jurors as she continued. "I will not be elaborating on these instructions, as they are the standard and any explanation I give may risk changing, rather than clarifying, the reasonable doubt standard." She replaced her glasses and focused on the document in front of her as she repeated word for word the instructions regarding reasonable doubt.

Omar glazed over the first time the judge read those instructions. This time he hung on every word. Certain phrases popped out at him and he hoped they struck home with the jury members too.

"… find the defendant not guilty, unless, on the evidence presented at this trial, you conclude that the People have proven the defendant guilty beyond a reasonable doubt… the defendant is not required to prove or disprove anything… the People must prove beyond a reasonable doubt every element of the crime including that the defendant is the person who committed that crime… a reasonable doubt is an honest doubt of the defendant's guilt…"

Omar watched the jurors faces as they focused on the judge. The presiding juror's jaw muscles twitched. Another frowned. Two yawned. Three jurors sat forward in their seats, appearing to hang on every word the judge uttered. Did they doubt a guilty or a not-guilty verdict? Omar sighed. This guessing game killed him. Which jurors leaned toward reasonable doubt and which ones didn't?

When the judge finished, the jury filed out and the courtroom erupted. Omar rose to search for Jahana. A space occupied her usual spot. Had she even shown up? He hadn't looked for her earlier, too absorbed in his own nerves. Maybe she'd returned to Ottawa, but he doubted it.

****

Once they made it past the swarm of reporters and settled into the living room, Didar turned on the TV. CNN blared in front of them. Omar rolled his eyes and left the room. That's all they listened to these days. He didn't need to relive each day in court repeatedly.

A familiar voice drifted into the hall, and he froze. He returned to the living room doorway and faced the TV. Jahana's face filled the screen.

"I believe beyond a reasonable doubt that Didar Fassid is guilty of the murder of Laurie Dalton. Even though the statute of limitations has passed, I think it is also obvious he raped her. Just like he raped my mother. In a dark alley, leaving her body bruised and torn without a thought for her safety. I live with the fact I'm the product of such a sexual assault every day. Do I believe he is still assaulting women? No, I don't. But that doesn't excuse him from what he's done in the past. It doesn't mean Laurie Dalton's family doesn't get the opportunity for closure. It doesn't mean Didar Fassid isn't punished for his actions."

Mahtob rose and brushed by Omar as she left the room. The bedroom door closed at the end of the hallway. He rounded the couch and sat on the chair opposite Didar. His grey pallor and expressionless eyes cut to Omar's soul. Didar picked up the remote and turned the TV off. He raised his head slowly and stared at Omar.

"The verdict might as well have been guilty in court today because the court of public opinion is convicting me. And my own flesh and blood is leading the charge."

Omar's heart weighed heavy; it couldn't hold any more sadness. There were no winners in this situation. The victims looked for closure, but his dad suffered even though he wasn't guilty. There was nothing left to say. Didar spoke the truth. Public opinion swayed to the prosecution's side. And Jahana made it her mission to ensure he paid for crimes he committed. He stared at his dad. A broken man. What was left to take from him?

Didar pushed himself up from his chair and shuffled off to bed.

CHAPTER TWENTY-THREE

Omar's parents talked in hushed tones behind their bedroom door. He hesitated. Should he eavesdrop? He didn't want to hear what they were talking about. Instead, he rapped on the door.

"I'm heading home. Everything all right?"

"Ah, yes, thanks Omar. Thanks for everything." Mahtob's voice rang out strong. Didar didn't respond. A knot formed in Omar's stomach. Didar rarely let Mahtob speak for him.

Omar battled his way through the reporters outside his parents' house and slid into his Porsche. When he arrived at his building, he drove into the underground parking area, avoiding the reporter vigil set up outside his building. He'd never leave through the front door again.

The faint aroma of dinner met him as he walked into the apartment and his stomach growled. The clock showed eight thirty, and he hadn't eaten since noon. Brie stepped around the corner. She must have seen the interview too. Without a word she slid her arms around his waist and laid her head on his chest. His breath caught in his throat, a lump forming, causing him to choke and gasp for air.

Brie didn't look up, she waited patiently. He put a hand over his mouth and rested his chin on her head, breathing in the inviting fragrance of coconut. *Oh, why can't we be somewhere tropical? Just the two of us. Can we run from this? Why not?*

Brie slid her hand into his and turned, leading him into the kitchen.

"Sit." She pointed to a bar stool. "I'll warm up some dinner for you, then we'll talk about it. For the moment breathe. That's all you have to do."

Omar grabbed a tissue from the top of the fridge before settling on the barstool, her words ringing in his ears. She was right. He only needed to breathe right now. Not think about Jahana and the people who believed her. He didn't need to relive the devastation in his dad's eyes. He didn't have to think about what this would do to their business. Closing his eyes, he breathed in and out.

His heartbeat and breathing slowed, and he concentrated on the air entering his nose and travelling down to his lungs, turning around and exiting through his mouth. The warm air brushed over his tongue and past his lips as his diaphragm relaxed.

When he opened his eyes, a glass of scotch sat in front of him and Brie held a plate from the microwave in her hand. She nodded toward the living room and he followed, glass in hand.

Once the last morsel had travelled from the plate to his mouth, Brie opened up.

"I waited to hear from you regarding the verdict. When you didn't call or text, I worried. But I found out on the news. And I'm sure the prosecutor's question bothers you a lot."

Omar gazed at her; his head tilted. "Doesn't it bother you?"

Brie nodded.

"And I'm sorry about not texting you. I planned to when we settled in at home, but Dad turned on CNN in time for us to watch Jahana stab him in the back again."

Brie avoided his eyes and clenched her teeth. "I understand why you didn't get in touch with me, but I wish you needed to talk to me and didn't see me as the person you had to keep informed."

Omar set his plate on the coffee table and held her close. "You are the person I need. Trust me. I'd be lost without you. I truly am sorry."

Brie nestled into his side, placing her hand on his chest over his heart.

Omar peered down at her. "It doesn't seem like Jahana's involvement with the prosecution bothers you."

"Of course, it does. I'm just not sure it's in the same way it bothers you."

Omar slid his arm out from around her and sat forward on the couch. "What do you mean, not in the same way?"

She averted her eyes. "Omar, why would Jahana do something like that if she didn't believe your dad was guilty? Is there something to her strong feelings? Has your dad done more than 'bad' things in his past? Maybe he's done terrible things."

Omar's eyes widened. "I thought you were on our side, Brie?"

Brie raised her head, looking into his eyes. "I'm a woman, Omar. I'm tired of the misogyny all around me. Women's voices aren't being heard. Men need to listen. It's time they're made accountable for their actions."

Omar's jaw dropped, and he stared at her, an ache building in his chest. "So, you think he's guilty?"

Brie's shoulder's sagged and she let out a long sigh. "I don't know Omar. How can you can be so certain he's not? Don't you have a little doubt?"

Omar sat in silence. She made him face the tiny box where he sent nagging doubts, locking them away. She made him turn the key, lift the lid and search inside.

"Honestly, I've had a few. But Brie, we're talking about Dad. He wouldn't do this."

"But what about all the times he's said he wasn't always the man he is today? What if that man did terrible things, like killing a woman in a drunken stupor?"

Omar threw his hands in the air and shook his head. "I can't accept that. Someone doesn't recover from murder and live a normal life, a good life."

"But what if he did? That's all I'm saying. There's a chance he did a terrible thing and doesn't even remember. But a woman died, and another woman claims Jahana's living proof of a rape. I'm not saying your dad's guilty. But I have doubts, that's all."

She wiped away a tear sliding down his cheek. "Whether or not he's guilty, it's out of our hands. Nothing we can do but wait for a verdict."

Omar brought her onto his lap and she rested her head on his chest. He didn't say it, but he had a plan. If Jahana could go public, so could he.

****

Omar lay awake. His phone showed 4:08 am. Brie slept beside him. He didn't want to wake her, but he needed to get out of bed. The turmoil over Jahana's interview on CNN ate at his soul. Time to do something.

He rose and crept to the study.

The glow of his laptop lit the room as it sprang to life. He pulled up a blog he used years ago and found his old password book at the back of his desk drawer. He logged in; the blog stared back at him.

What did he plan to do exactly? If he called CNN and asked for an interview, he'd get it. But he'd appear petty and might not keep his cool, depending on their questions. People thought his dad was guilty, it didn't look good. But they didn't know him. If he wrote a blog explaining the respect, his dad had for women, would it help?

He clicked on 'new post' and typed. It started as a conscious stream of thought, but after several revisions he re-read it aloud. Did it portray the dad he knew?

You see my dad as a man sitting in a courtroom on charges of murder, but you don't see him through my eyes.

My dad dances with my mother in the kitchen. He has for as long as I can remember. Sometimes there's music playing, sometimes there's not.

Our house smells of flowers, their scent permeating the walls from thirty-seven years of weekly bouquets. Every week my dad walks in the house with flowers behind his back, like it's a big surprise. He wraps my mom in a one-armed hug, and pulls away as she tears away the florist's paper and lets out a magical sigh like it's the first time he has ever bought her flowers.

My dad's eyes reflect the reverence he has for my mom. Their love is palpable.

This is the man being convicted by public opinion for the murder he's fighting in court, but other crimes against women he hasn't even been charged with haunt him as well. Crimes he didn't and couldn't commit. Unfair judgements.

I have grown up learning respect for women from him, through his words and his actions toward my mother, his employees, my girlfriend and every other woman he has come in contact with.

Until you've walked a mile in my dad's shoes, I ask you to reserve judgement. Didar's not the man you've conjured him to be.

The cursor hovered over the publish key and he pressed the mouse before losing his nerve. He linked the post to a tweet targeted at CNN and closed his laptop before padding back down the hall and sliding into bed. Brie hadn't moved. At last he found solace in sleep.

****

Omar woke after noon, alone in the apartment. He hadn't heard Brie leave for work. With coffee in hand, he dug his toes into the shag rug, settled into the couch and picked up his phone. It sprang to life with alerts of text messages and missed calls. He turned on CNN. Scrolling across the bottom of the screen the newsfeed read: Fassid's son calls for understanding. His heart quickened. His post flashed on the screen.

"In the early hours of this morning Omar Fassid, son of Didar Fassid, the man charged with the murder of Laurie Dalton, posted this blog appealing to the public to believe his dad is not guilty…"

Omar parted the curtains and peeked out the window. The media lined the street. The blood drained from his face. Had he done the right thing? He doubted his parents would agree with his post. He glanced again at his missed calls and texts, choosing to call Brie first.

"Well if it isn't the most popular guy on CNN?"

"Just woke up. I had no idea all of this was going on?" Omar settled on the couch.

"Well what did you think would happen? Why didn't you tell me what you were planning to do?" Brie spoke softly, but her voice held an edge.

"Why is it bad? I've got CNN on TV but so far they're droning on, not saying much of anything."

"Well it's not all bad. There seems to be a mix of support and hatred. But there are a lot of angry women speaking up saying your dad doesn't respect women, and you, by association, don't either. But there are some people saying you're right to stand up for your father and others feel sorry for you."

Omar felt the rise and fall of his chest. "Sorry I didn't tell you. It came to me in the middle of the night when I couldn't sleep. I had to counteract Jahana's interview."

Brie's voice softened. "You were trying to help, but you've stirred people up."

"Maybe that's good. They need stirring up. It's time we stopped sitting by and letting the prosecution sway public opinion. Why can't people see there's two sides here?"

Brie didn't reply. An awkward silence filled the air. She cleared her throat before she replied. "People say the same thing about you, Omar. Why can't you see the victim's side?"

"Really Brie? I thought you understood." He hung up the phone. Brie called back, but he turned it over, picked up his coffee and turned up CNN. Time to face the music.

****

Jahana lay in bed, room service dishes on the floor beside her. After Baba watched her interview on TV, he begged her to come home, but she couldn't leave. She needed to see this trial through to the end which meant staying until the jury reached a verdict. She extended her absence from work using personal reasons.

She understood their concern, but so far, the hotel provided a safe haven, and she hoped it would stay that way. The room service delivery staff stared at her, but no one bothered her. She lived in a bubble of safety.

The pit of her stomach turned when she thought about Omar. He doted on his dad, looking past his faults with no consideration of his transgressions. He conjured up heartwarming memories on his blog, but Jahana sensed they were just the veneer coating some hideous stories Omar may not remember or even know about.

Mahtob's reaction in the bathroom haunted her. How did she not doubt her husband? There must be memories of things that didn't seem right filling her with doubt of his innocence. But in court she sat stoic behind her man, never wavering.

The awful comments on CNN and posted to Omar's blog made her sick to her stomach. Why hadn't he adjusted his settings to moderate the blog comments and ensure they were appropriate before being published? And it had been hours since he'd posted, why didn't he fix it now?

She opened her laptop and navigated to the comments section. As much as she liked the support, she couldn't tolerate the hatred towards Omar. Didar was the perpetrator, not him. She needed to do something to quell the haters.

> *Perspective is reality. Sometimes it's difficult to consider the other side when the lens you've peered through is coloured a certain way from experiences or influences in your life. Passions are high. My brother is only giving his perspective on this very controversial situation and asking for it to be considered. I'm sorry he has to go through any of this, just like I'm sorry the victim had to go through what she went through and the family has had to live without knowing what happened to her for almost 40 years. There's a lot of hurt on all sides. Can we all try to practice a little understanding?*

Jahana reread her words. Were they okay? She hoped so as she hit the publish button. There'd already been too much hurt.

****

Omar opened his blog. He should have moderated the comments, but he hadn't been thinking. The most recent comment was from Jahana. While he appreciated her attempt to thwart the haters, she didn't acknowledge the pain his mom and dad were being put through. What happened to innocent until proven guilty?

He clicked on reply and typed a response.

> *What happened to innocent until proven guilty? My dad is supposed to be presumed innocent. Why are we fighting so hard to prove innocence? It is not up to anyone to point fingers and blame. We are going through a trial. The jurors will serve justice when they declare a not-guilty verdict.*

Brie's words echoed in his ear. *Well what did you think would happen?* He didn't care. The arrow of the mouse hovered, then he clicked publish.

Immediately comments appeared. Some comforting, most not. If this is the way the public felt, he worried the jury would sway in the same direction. He fumbled with the setting menu. It had been a long time since he blogged. Figuring out how to stop comments from publishing without approval took him awhile.

He pushed back from the computer and stood, stretching. The weight gain and aches and pains from not making time to work out caught up with him. It was impossible with the media hounding him. Brie left him a plate of pancakes and bacon before going to work. Perfect comfort food.

He added maple syrup to the pancakes before putting the plate in the microwave. It was the maple syrup Jahana had given him the first time they met. That seemed like such a long time ago.

He settled at the kitchen table, recognizing the couch and syrup weren't a good combination. CNN wafted in from the living room. The news looped back to his story. Syrup or no syrup, he had to watch. He rose and took his plate into the living room, standing in the middle of the floor, syrup dripping off his fork to the plate. At least no one witnessed the level he'd stooped to.

An update scrolled across the screen. They had Jahana's comment and his reply. *Boy they don't waste any time.* Is this really the most exciting thing happening in the world right now? An expert analyzed their words. What next? He'd had enough and shut the TV off returning to the kitchen to place the dirty plate in the sink.

In his study, he faced his computer screen once more and hit the delete button. *Brie, you were right, what was I thinking?*

He picked up the phone and dialled his dad. Time to face the music. At least he'd taken the blog down. What a crappy idea.

CHAPTER TWENTY-FOUR

N o, no, there's never been bed bugs."

Omar peered up at his father and tugged on his sleeve, but his dad shot him a look that said, *Not now.*

But there had been bed bugs. Omar remembered it clear as day. A company fumigated the apartment and the condo board agreed to fumigate the common areas. No one knew where they had come from. It wasn't more than a few months ago. He could still taste the residue of chemicals when he first walked in. Surely his dad hadn't forgotten?

But he waited until the potential new renters left and they were on the way home before he asked the question eating him up inside.

"Why did you lie about the bedbugs, Dad?"

Didar reached out and patted his knee. "Sometimes lying is necessary. I only told a little white lie. We killed the bedbugs. There's no need to worry potential renters."

"But how does that differ from me skipping school? You told me that was lying, and it hurt you."

"That's the difference, Son. The lie I told today won't hurt anyone. The lie you told did."

Omar remained silent and contemplated letting the subject drop. "But skipping wouldn't have hurt you either if you hadn't found out. If the bedbugs return, it will hurt them."

Didar smiled. "You're a clever one. Maybe you should be a lawyer when you grow up. Knowing when it's okay to lie is a skill you learn as you experience things in life through trial and error. You're too young to understand, but you get a feeling in your stomach that guides you so you know when it's okay to lie. Most of the time, you should tell the truth though. Remember that. The truth will set you free, as they say."

Omar sat in silence the rest of the way home. He'd never heard his dad lie before. And it didn't feel good. That feeling his dad described, was sitting in the pit of his stomach.

When he walked through the door, he smelled stew cooking in the slow cooker, but he didn't feel like eating.

"Omar come eat. It's getting cold."

"I don't feel good. I'm going to lie on my bed for a while." While in his room he heard his parents talking.

"What happened today?"

"Oh, he just heard me tell the potential tenants the place never had bedbugs. He had lots of questions about lying. But I had to. If we tell anyone about the bedbugs, we'll never get renters."

"He hangs on your every word. I'll go talk to him."

"No leave him be. He needs to come to terms with the fact that people can't tell the truth all the time. We're fallible. He'll come around when he gets hungry enough."

Omar lay staring at the ceiling. Would he ever be able to come to terms with the fact his dad wasn't perfect? That he lied once in a while?

A few hours later he opened his bedroom door and ventured into the kitchen where he warmed a bowl of stew and joined his parents in the living room.

Didar never mentioned lying again.

CHAPTER TWENTY-FIVE

Didar lay in bed, but didn't rest. The blood pounded in his ears. Mahtob insisted he lay down after Omar's phone call and suggested an Ativan. He gave in and took one. Something needed to calm him down before Omar arrived.

Was his world truly going to fall apart? Would he spend the rest of his life behind bars?

"Can I get you anything?" Mahtob popped her head in the door. How did he deserve her? He spent a lifetime asking himself that question without an answer. Especially now.

"No, I'm fine. The Ativan's working."

"Try not to be too hard on Omar. He tried to help."

Didar shook his head and waved his hand at her. "I know, I know."

***

Didar awoke with a start. Voices drifted in from the hallway, too low to make out the words. Where was he? What day was it? Then it came flooding back. He relished the first seconds after waking. It was when everything was as he had built it. A life where he paid for previous sins on his terms and no one had to know what those sins were. Reality hit like a long fall, hard and unforgiving.

He sat up in bed; the room spun. Ativan did its job. The door opened a crack and Omar peeked in.

"Hey, you're awake. Can I come in?"

"Son come in. Don't mind me but Ativan has sent me for a loop. I'm just going to lie back down. Pull up that chair and have a seat."

Didar rubbed his temples, willing the fogginess to lift. Omar settled in.

"Sorry I upset you Dad, and sorry about writing the blog post. I've taken it down, but the damage is done. I've created more publicity and controversy. Most people were talking about your case before the post, but now it seems everyone is talking about it."

"It's one of your stupider moves." Didar stopped rubbing his temples and glanced at Omar, a smile playing at the corners of his mouth.

"Can't disagree. But Dad, I meant what I wrote. You set a good example. I only hope Brie and I can emulate the love you and Mom have." Omar glanced at his dad.

Didar stared at the ceiling. "Relationships aren't easy and I haven't always been good at them, that's for sure. Your mother gets all the credit for turning me into the man I am. And you as well. When you made me a father, I viewed life through different eyes."

Omar made a few false starts before broaching the question truly weighing on his mind. "You've always hinted at a past you'd rather forget. And many times, over my lifetime you've hinted at bad deeds. Do you truly not remember Laurie Dalton?"

Didar rubbed his forehead and readjusted his pillow. "Son, no, I do not remember Laurie Dalton. Am I sorry for whatever happened to her? Absolutely. But I'm not capable of killing anyone. If something happened to her in my presence, I would have done something about it. Her head did not hit that brick while I was there. I wish I remembered something from that night."

Didar continued to stare at the ceiling, not once meeting Omar's stare.

"Dad, remember the time a woman threw a drink at you in a bar and you said she was a stranger?"

Didar chuckled. "Yeah, I remember. What a piece of work."

"Well the next morning I ran into her in the hotel gym. She came in as I was leaving and insisted you assaulted her. Are you sure you never met her?"

"What are you saying, Son?"

"I guess… I guess I'm saying that it seems like this keeps coming up. And you keep your past secret. What do you expect me to believe? I'm conflicted. You're a generous, respectful, kind man and the best father I could ask for, but then you cloak your past in mystery and three women say you assaulted them. No matter what Dad, I'll stand beside you. I just want to know the truth."

Didar stared at Omar. His face emotionless; some might say stoic. "I didn't do it, Son. I swear."

Didar closed his eyes and breathed. Omar held his hand.

"Okay Dad. I believe you. No need to get that blood pressure up again."

When he opened his eyes, Omar had left. Didar felt a weight heavy on his chest.

His son's doubt hurt.

****

Omar swirled his fifth glass of scotch when Brie's key turned in the door. His phone buzzed several times, but he didn't pick up. The more he drank, the more palpable her betrayal from the other night. He thought he could work through it, but she figuratively crossed the courtroom floor and like everyone else tried to hang his dad for a crime he didn't commit.

"Omar?"

"In here." Omar sat in the chair opposite the sofa, he didn't bother to rise when she entered the room and sat stiffly on the couch. Another swig of scotch, slid down slowly, leaving a good burn in its wake.

"Omar, I'm worried. Why wouldn't you take my calls?" She leaned forward.

"Oh, I don't know, maybe your accusation that I have no empathy for the victim's family had something to do with it? Really Brie? Do you think I'm heartless?" He watched the scotch swirl in the bottom of the glass, grateful he'd poured a generous amount. He tipped the glass back and took another mouthful, this time letting it dance on his tongue before swallowing the burn.

"How much have you had to drink? Should I even try to talk to you right now?" Brie slid forward on the couch.

"I've had enough to deaden my fears. The ones where my dad might go to jail for a crime he didn't commit." Omar swirled his glass, the ice tinkling as the scotch eddied.

"But how do you know for sure? Like I said, your dad talked about a past where he wasn't the man he is today. Maybe in those days he could rape and murder someone?"

Omar set his glass on the side table and leaned forward, staring into Brie's eyes. "He never was that kind of man. We talked about those very things today and he assured me he's innocent. And I believe him Brie. I have to. Why can't you?"

"Omar, I've always liked your dad. He's been good to me. But he's also stared at me when no one else was watching, causing chills to run up my spine. I chalked it up to irrational thoughts. But when he was charged, something clicked. A woman should always listen to her intuition."

Omar stared, his jaw gaping. "My father gives you an uncomfortable feeling? Are you kidding?"

"Not always, Omar, just sometimes. I can't explain it. I haven't accompanied you to court because I'm not sure my expression wouldn't give me away."

Omar studied his hands; white knuckles clasped his glass between his knees. He leaned forward, head bent, slowly raising his gaze to meet Brie's. "You need to leave." The words caught in his throat and came out in distinct syllables.

Brie's eyes filled with tears and she tried to grasp his hands. He set his glass on the end table and batted her hands away, rising and walking past her into the kitchen. He returned to the empty living room with the scotch bottle.

Sobs floated down the stairs as dresser drawers slammed and suitcase zippers closed. He picked up his glass and poured himself another finger, settling back into the chair. It might be the booze, but Brie needed to leave. He couldn't live with someone who makes insinuations about his father.

"Maybe you did learn how to respect women from your father after all." The words escaped into the room and down the hall as the front door closed quietly, a wisp of air escaping with something precious. Omar lifted the glass to his lips. The light caught the glint of white gold and diamond before it slid towards his lips. The mouthful of amber liquid flowed back into the glass and down his chin. A silent wail erupted from his lips. This time she was gone for good.

****

Jahana contemplated hanging up when she heard Omar's strangled voice. She glanced at the clock, ten after one. Had she really just woken him?

Switching the phone to her other hand she sat up straighter in the hotel desk chair. Sadness replaced the anger over the blog. "Omar, thank you for taking my call. I worried you wouldn't."

"I'm surprised you're calling. After my blog I thought you'd never speak to me again." He coughed into the phone.

"Why would you think that? You must have seen my response. Did I wake you? You sound terrible."

Jahana didn't like what she heard. His voice was full of gravel and exhaustion.

"Yeah, I'm fine. Just had a bit too much to drink last night."

"Oh okay." Something told her his voice held more than the remnants of a hangover, but she let it go. "Thank you for taking down your blog."

"Well it really didn't benefit me much. Seemed like it garnered more support for my dad's haters than helping people understand who he really is."

Jahana paused, not sure she wanted to continue. "You don't have any doubts? You've said your dad has regrets in life. Could sexual assault and murder not be some of those regrets? Please try to help me understand your unwavering support."

Omar seemed to choose his words carefully. "My dad's not perfect, no one is. He's alluded to an imperfect past on several occasions. For the most part I've only seen people love him, but there've been a few occasions where they've shown anger toward him. Those moments gave me pause. But when I've asked my dad about the anger, he's been able to explain it. There is one incident in particular when a woman threw a drink at my dad in a bar and later told me he assaulted her. But my dad doesn't remember her and I think she had the wrong man."

"Are you kidding? Another woman? How many women have to come forward? And how long can your dad keep using a bad memory as an excuse?" Jahana struggled to keep the emotion out of her voice, but it crept in.

"He drank a lot in the old days. Booze can take away your memory and make you do things you wish you hadn't. I'm not saying he did nothing wrong, but he didn't do what he's being accused of."

"Like you said, booze can make you do things you regret." Jahana shifted in her chair and eyed the bed as a more comfortable option.

"But booze wouldn't make him murder anyone. When he drinks, he's a happy person, not aggressive. Besides, he cleaned up his life. He's been a good person, giving back every chance he gets. He raised me with good values and has been a good husband. What would putting him in jail do?" A raspy cough escaped into the phone.

"Let's suspend your belief he's innocent for a minute. If he raped and murdered Laurie Dalton, shouldn't he be punished?" Jahana moved to the bed and piled up pillows before laying down.

"He's punished himself for years, whether it was for murder and rape or lesser things. He's reformed. Jail will not make a different man out of him."

Jahana paused. "But it's not just about reforming. It's about facing up to what he's done. It's about being punished. He has owned none of it. He's had a nice life. It's his victims that have dealt with the consequences all these years. He's just moved on."

"Doesn't being a good person, instilling good values in his son, being a good husband pay society back for anything he might have done? Why isn't that enough?"

Jahana forced herself to swallow before answering, struggling to keep the emotion out of her voice. "Because he's not taking responsibility, he's not allowing his victims to move on. He's not giving Laurie Dalton's family closure."

"But what if he didn't do it? Let's suspend your belief that he did. What if he had sex with Laurie Dalton and left her inebriated and she fell and hit her head on the brick? Think about what this court case is doing to him."

Jahana lost patience. How could Omar not get it? "But the evidence is stacked against him. And what about keeping his word to me? He made a deal. I gave him a kidney, and he lied to me. How can you trust his word? Why would an innocent man agree to the deal in the first place? It speaks to his character and you need to face the facts. Your father is not reformed. He's just become a fantastic con man. He's had years to perfect it." Jahana took a breath before continuing her rant.

Omar interrupted. "I won't convince you of my dad's innocence and you'll never convince me he's guilty. I'm sorry you can't see our side of this situation." Omar's voice shook.

"And I'm sorry you're blind to the truth. No matter how much your dad has reformed, he's never paid for the crimes he's committed. In my mind, and in the minds of the other women who see him for what he truly is, he needs to go to jail. He needs to own his actions."

A hollow spot expanded inside Jahana. There was nothing else to say, so she hung up.

CHAPTER TWENTY-SIX

"Who's that?" Omar pointed a chubby finger at the black and white photo. Cuddled up to his dad on the couch, he explored an old album. The two of them scanned these pages hundreds of times, but something different always jumped out at him. The stories his dad told were the best part. Tehran seemed like such a fairy tale. Without the pictures he'd never have believed it ever happened.

"That's Taavi, my only brother. His name means 'adored'. And he was. My parents did anything for him."

Omar leaned over to get a closer look, then glanced up at his dad. "He looks like you."

Didar chuckled. "People used to say that. We were less than two years apart. Lots of people mistook us for twins. In that picture he was about twelve."

"What happened to him? Why haven't I met him?" Omar reached out and touched the photograph, running his finger over Taavi.

"He died in Iran during the revolution. I always teased him, saying he was like a cat, had nine lives. But I guess he used them up early."

"What do you mean? How did he use up his lives?"

"Oh, there were lots of childhood accidents, boys being boys. There was the time he fell out of a tree and broke his collarbone. And the time he stayed in the hospital because a dog bit him and he ended up with a terrible infection. Even as an adult trouble followed him. The year before his execution he caused a terrible accident."

"What happened?"

"He hit a boy while driving. He'd been drinking, but somehow my dad kept that detail out of court. It was the boy's father who decided if he would hang. Lucky for Taavi, he forgave him and Taavi didn't even go to jail. When the boy's father talked about the power of forgiveness, I was in court. He said if he didn't forgive Taavi, it would be like a cancer that ate at him and his family. By not forgiving he wouldn't be able to move on. It was an accident, and he talked about how we all do things we wish we hadn't, and didn't see the sense for another person to suffer. There'd been suffering enough." Didar leaned back into the couch, staring into nothing.

"Wow, that's amazing. If someone killed me, would you be able to forgive them?" Omar turned away from the picture and met his dad's gaze.

Didar snapped out of his reverie. "That's a great question. I don't think it's something you know until you're faced with the situation. I think I'd find it in my heart to forgive. Forgiveness is something I try to practice a lot because of what that man said. Forgiveness is about setting yourself free, more than about setting the other person free. Although it achieves both."

"If someone killed you, I can't imagine being able to forgive them." Anger seeped into Omar's voice.

"I hope you could, Son. I'd want you to."

CHAPTER TWENTY-SEVEN

Didar eyed Jahana a few steps ahead of them, fighting the throngs of reporters. When they entered the foyer, he turned to escape through the side doors to the courtroom. The doors the media couldn't enter. Jahana tried to push her way through the reporters.

"Omar, go rescue Jahana, she can come with us." Didar pointed in Jahana's direction and Omar grabbed her sleeve, pulling her towards them. They ducked through the side door; the roar of the media quieted by the oak door closing.

"Thank you," Jahana mumbled to Omar before lowering her eyes.

Didar swallowed. It couldn't have worked better. He would get a chance to talk to her before heading into court. It would be his last chance. The jury deliberated for over a week and were at last ready to deliver a verdict. At least he hoped they were, and this didn't turn into another question period.

The four of them walked in silence toward the courtroom. As they approached, Didar turned to Jahana.

"Can I have a word with you?"

Jahana's face flushed. "Alone?"

"Yes, if you don't mind. I'd like to explain a few things. Omar, Mahtob, please go in. I'll be right there."

Jahana turned up the hallway that would take her to the foyer outside the courtroom and waited. Omar and Mahtob entered the courtroom, and the door closed behind them. She stood against the wall; arms folded.

Didar stepped forward. "Look, I might not have a chance to talk to you again. I'm sorry for all you've gone through. I don't blame you for not believing me and for hating me for not keeping my word."

Jahana raised her gaze to meet his. He searched for some hint of forgiveness, but didn't find it.

"Regardless of the outcome today, please know I didn't murder anyone. Although I don't remember that night, I wouldn't have killed her."

Jahana's stone faced expression didn't waver. Nor did it appear she had any intention of speaking.

Didar studied the floor and cleared his throat. "Ah, and I'm sorry for what your mother went through. I don't remember her, which doesn't say much about who I was as a young man. But I'm no longer that person. I never raped anyone, even as a young pompous entitled ass. Sex was always consensual."

Jahana took a deep breath, but remained silent.

Didar reached into his blazer pocket. "I have something for you. I'm glad I have a chance to give it to you. If we didn't have this encounter, I would have asked Omar to pass it on." Didar held out a cheque. "I want you to have this. It's not an admission of guilt, but it's payment for being an absent father. For all the times I wasn't there for you. You made a great sacrifice. Consider it a small token of my appreciation and attempt at reimbursement for the things I didn't pay for in your lifetime."

His hand shook as he held the cheque between them. She glanced down and her eyes widened. She looked up to meet his stare, arms folded in front of her.

Didar stepped closer. "Please take it. It's not absolution from the things you believe I've done. It's a father trying to make amends."

Jahana's weight shift as she straightened and reached out to take the cheque. *She can't resist half a million dollars.* He smiled and already felt better knowing the rest of her life would be easier.

"Someday I'll regret this." Jahana continued to stare into his eyes, her voice low. "There's no compensation that will pay for what you've done to my mother, to Laurie Dalton and to who knows how many others. You've spent your life trying to pay for your sins by moving forward, but you don't get it. The one thing you need to do, you refuse to do. You won't own up to your sins, apologize to your victims, give them the opportunity to heal and get some closure." Jahana raised her hands in exasperation. "You're a good dad to Omar and a good husband to Mahtob. But take responsibility for your past actions. Using money or good deeds to right wrongs doesn't absolve you for past deeds."

Didar sighed. She'd never believe his innocence.

Jahana stared at the cheque, then glanced back at him. She folded the cheque and ripped it into small pieces, letting them fall to the floor. She turned and walked away. Didar shifted his gaze from the pieces on the floor to Jahana's back. There was nothing left to say. He knelt down, picked up the pieces and watched Jahana exit the door at the end of the hallway.

Didar grasped the door knob to the courtroom, took a deep breath and entered; the shredded cheque weighed heavy in his pocket.

****

The side door to the courtroom opened and Omar's father stumbled as he crossed the floor to the defence table; his face pale and drawn. *Had he looked that way earlier? Or did his appearance change after talking with Jahana? What did she say?*

Omar turned in time to see Jahana enter the courtroom. She stared straight ahead and settled into her usual spot behind the victim's family, resting her hand on the mother's shoulder. Jahana adopted another family.

Why couldn't she try to be part of his? Why did that hurt so much? He didn't need a sister. Yet he longed for her to fill that role.

Once settled, she turned and their eyes met. He smiled, she pursed her lips and averted her gaze to the front of the courtroom. Whatever they discussed; it didn't assuage her anger.

She glanced at him one more time, giving him the courage needed to stand and cross the aisle. He crouched down beside her and rested his hand on hers.

"Jahana, I'm sorry this is so difficult. Please come sit with us?"

The victim's mother turned and glared. Her hair as white as the pearl necklace she wore. He searched Jahana's face imploring her to cross the aisle. Her hand slid out from under his, their eyes locked.

Her lips barely moved. "I'm where I want to be. Please return to your seat. You're making everyone uncomfortable."

Omar rose, bowed his head and returned to sit next to his mother. She reached across and squeezed his hand.

"All rise."

Didar stood in front of them. His lawyer leaned over and whispered something then raised his eyebrows. Didar nodded and smiled. *What was that all about?* Didar supported himself on the table in front of him, hunched over. This wasn't like him. He always stood tall and straight. *What's wrong?*

"Please be seated."

Didar fell into his chair.

"Does the jury have a verdict?"

The silence in the courtroom sat heavy. Omar held his breath.

The head juror rose and faced the judge. "We do your honour."

Didar gripped the sides of his chair. Was he bracing against the words that would determine the rest of his life?

"Could the defendant please rise."

Didar grabbed the table and pulled himself to his feet. His lawyer seemed oblivious to his dad's struggle. Omar turned to Mahtob, she glanced back her eyes wide with alarm. Something was wrong.

Omar returned his attention back to his dad in time to see him crumple to the floor, his head just missing the table on his way down. The room erupted into chaos.

The judge's gavel pounded as Omar stepped over the railing. Bailiffs dragged him back. Mahtob wailed. The lawyer punched numbers on his phone, presumably 911. Paramedics burst through the doors and headed straight to Didar.

With trembling knees Omar lowered himself to the bench and leaned his head on the rail.

Mahtob tapped him on the shoulder. "They're taking him to Mount Sinai."

The stretcher wheeled past Omar and out of the courtroom. The judge's gavel tried to restore order before she announced recess, reconvening when Mr. Fassid is up to it.

Omar raced across the aisle, blocking Jahana's exit.

"What did you say to him!"

Jahana picked up her purse, avoiding his eyes. "Not a thing. He did most of the talking." She pushed past Omar and walked out of the courtroom. Mahtob grabbed his elbow and steered him out.

"Calm down Omar. You're making a scene."

He glared at his mother and between clenched teeth responded. "It's her fault."

"We don't know that Omar. Calm down. We need to get to the hospital. Call for the car."

Omar punched out the driver's number and growled into the phone. "We're leaving now, how far away are you?"

"I'm still outside. Thought I'd wait here. I saw the ambulance. Everything okay?"

"No, it's not. We'll be going to Mount Sinai hospital. We're on our way out."

Omar took a deep breath, grabbed his mother's elbow and steered her through the swarm of reporters who for the first time stepped aside and let them by. *They are human after all.*

Omar shielded his eyes from the sun's glare. The car remained where they left it. He opened the door for Mahtob then ran to the other side and slid in beside her. He closed the door, and Mahtob's outburst filled the air.

"What the hell was that all about?" Her arms flailed in exasperation.

"Sorry, I lost my cool. But isn't it strange that Dad's fine, talks to Jahana and then collapses in court? She said or did something to upset him. You could see it in his eyes when he walked into the courtroom."

"Your dad asked to talk to her. I'm not defending her, but your dad may have brought this on himself. I caught him writing a cheque this morning. When I asked what it was for, he slipped it in his pocket and ignored my question. Something happened all right, but your dad started it. As much as I'd like to blame Jahana, we can't."

Omar rested his head in his hands as buildings slid by.

CHAPTER TWENTY-EIGHT

They moved in slow motion. Is this how it would end? He gave up everything for his father; his fiancé, his sister, his life. And now his dad would die before they even had a verdict? What had the past months been about? What if he rejected Jahana's kidney? He'd fought too hard to save his father, first with a kidney then with a defence. Is couldn't end like this.

Didar lay on a stretcher in the emergency department hallway. He had an IV started and someone took his blood. His colour was much improved.

"Dad, what happened?" Relief washed over Omar.

"Oh, I fainted, not sure why. But I'm feeling better already. Don't look so worried. It's not serious. Wish I lasted till they read the verdict. Now we have to go through it all again."

"Thank God Dad. We didn't come this far to end in a tragedy. You'll win this thing and get your life back."

"Omar, I doubt we'll ever get our lives back. The court of public opinion has already declared me guilty. Nothing will ever be the same."

"Oh Dad, this will die down. Maybe we should move somewhere else?"

"No, Son, running is not an option. Things will die down, but they'll always call me the guy who got away with murder." Didar paused; his voice much quieter. "Unless I spend the rest of my life in jail."

Omar glanced at his mom. She stroked Didar's hand. "Well let's concentrate on getting you well enough to face that verdict."

But Didar hoped they'd put it off a little longer. This might be the calm before the storm.

****

When they arrived at court, Jahana sat in her usual spot. She wouldn't meet Omar's gaze. Jahana hadn't reached out to ask how Didar was, but she would have heard the media reports. Initially it was reported Didar had a stroke or a heart attack, but they eventually reported the truth; his blood pressure caused him to faint. He had a bump on his head where he hit the floor, but other than that, his blood pressure was back down and he had a clean bill of health. And the news reported it as that.

The courtroom buzzed with speculation about what the verdict would be. Omar scanned the jurors; most of them wouldn't meet his eye. One man stared at him, but as soon as their eyes locked, he glanced down. Omar's stomach churned. This wouldn't go the way they hoped.

"Mr. Fassid, if it's better for you, please remain seated while I read the verdict. If you feel well enough, you may rise."

All eyes turned to Didar. Omar knew his dad would stand. His pride would force him to rise. True to form, Didar pushed his chair back and stood. This time he stood tall and clasped his hands behind his back, as if it was a day like every other.

Omar sighed. Mahtob reached over and placed her hand on his.

The judge droned on about technicalities, then she uttered the words. "On the charge of first-degree murder, how does the jury find the defendant?"

The pause was excruciating. Omar wanted it over with and yet he didn't. He wasn't religious, but he bowed his head that morning and asked God to return his dad home. He hadn't talked to God since he was a little boy. It didn't seem right to ask for something so big, when he didn't even know if he believed in God. Would God laugh in his face? But he recalled part of a scripture from when he attended catholic school. *My power is made perfect in weakness.* If that were true, the helplessness and weakness would feed God's power. At any rate, the scripture gave him strength to ask a God, he had all but forgotten about, for a huge favour.

The judge's words hung in the air. The courtroom remained silent. Someone at the back coughed. Omar watched the head juror stand and face his dad from the jury box. He shifted from one foot to the other. The paper holding Didar's fate shook in his hands. He avoided looking at Didar. Omar's heart sunk.

"Your honour, on the charge of first-degree murder, we find the defendant, Didar Fassid, not guilty."

The words rang in Omar's ears. *Not guilty*. He turned to his mom. Tears streamed down her cheeks. His dad's head bowed, and he turned striding over to Mahtob. He reached out and cradled her cheeks in both hands, searching her eyes. A slow smile spread across his face. He held back tears.

Omar regarded the victim's parents. They sat in heaps, distraught, tears falling along with their hopes. His heart ached for them. But the prosecution hadn't proven beyond a reasonable doubt his dad murdered their daughter. Jahana consoled them. He wished he could too.

Jahana's eyes met his; the anger palpable. She shook her head in disbelief, then stood and marched through the courtroom and out the door. *Would he ever see her again?* His heart dropped.

Arms surrounded him and the tears his dad had been struggling to keep under control, flowed. His breath coming out in gasps and words of thank you blurted in staccato.

Omar didn't cry. He remained calm. Too many mixed emotions filled his heart to react. His dad was free, yet the victim's family would forever be at a loss to explain how their daughter died. And Jahana, the sister he found so late in life, might never speak to him again. And Brie... He had to stop himself there. Thinking of Brie would tip him over the edge.

It was like walking along a cliff where the easiest way down would be to jump. But he'd stay where he was. A good son, supporting his father. That's what his parents taught him. Family meant everything.

CHAPTER TWENTY-NINE

Omar watched his dad slide into a growing malaise. Something deeper, more profound than damaged kidneys was killing him. A month after the verdict and Didar hadn't stepped out the front door. The press hung around for two weeks, but even they gave up hope Didar would appear in public. They arranged for a doctor to visit, alleviating the need for regular visits to the hospital.

"Omar, can you pick up a few groceries later? I'm just putting together a list. It might be nice to make Tabbouleh, but I need more parsley." Mahtob glanced up as Omar entered the kitchen. She still put on makeup and did her hair every day, even though she rarely left the house.

After the trial, Omar fell into the role of errand boy. In fact, he did everything for his parents, grocery shopping, yard work, Christ he'd even delivered urine samples to the lab. He didn't mind, his parents had done so much for him. He offered to stop by Lana's flower shop, but Didar abruptly declared there would be no more flowers purchased from Lana. It was strange not see a bouquet in the house, but his mom didn't seem to mind.

The dead gaze in his father's eyes was what really bothered Omar. It crushed his soul. And he wondered if his acts of love enabled his father's depression.

"Sure mom. I have a conference call a little later, but I can go after that." Mahtob patted his cheek as he grabbed a cookie cooling on the counter and sauntered out of the kitchen.

Business slowed; they were forced to downsize. The press coverage of the trial prompted most of their customers to seek out their competition. Only a few loyal ones remained. Many employees quit, and because of the decrease in business, Omar laid a few off. Business was down to bare bones. He tried to re-imagine the business: a new market, a new name. But it became nothing more than a distraction. Didar hadn't asked about the business since the trial. His life's work crumbled, and he didn't need to be told about it.

Omar entered the dining room. He noticed her picture sitting inside the cabinet. How had he missed it before? Brie stared back at him, a mischievous grin on her face. His stomach clenched. *Don't be ridiculous. It's time to get over it.* He hadn't seen or heard from Brie since she moved back in with Kathy. She distanced herself from the Fassid name. Deep down he was relieved she escaped the media circus.

Omar reached into the cabinet and moved the small framed photo to the back out of view.

Jahana hadn't been as lucky as Brie. She found herself caught in the middle of it all. And he blamed himself for that. A piece of him hoped she'd keep in touch, but he phoned once and she didn't pick up or call back. Text messages remained unanswered. She'd severed ties to them. The last time he saw her she gave an interview outside the courtroom the day of the verdict. It replayed on TV for the next few days. Anger seethed through her words. She remained adamant justice had not been served and Didar was guilty, although she conceded he didn't pose a danger to society. She reiterated how he never took responsibility for his actions. Never gave his victims or their families closure. She wanted him punished for the crimes she still believed he committed. Omar didn't agree with Jahana's assessment. He watched his dad punish himself every day.

Omar stood in the living room doorway; Didar slouched in a chair with a game show blaring on the TV.

Some days his dad stayed in bed till noon, never showered or changed out of pajamas. He sat comatose in front of the TV watching whatever came on. Not bothering to search for something interesting. Omar encouraged him to see a doctor. But Didar didn't believe in depression or the pills that might alleviate it. Besides seeing a doctor about depression might mean leaving the house. On good days he slipped out the back door and puttered in the garden. But a few minutes later he returned to his chair in front of the TV.

Omar turned down the hall towards the stairs that descended to his living quarters. He sold his condo and moved into the basement a few weeks before. Who would have thought this is where he'd be at thirty-four years old? He told himself it would only be until the public forgot about his dad. But he wondered if they'd ever forget. He paused at the top of the stairs and returned to the living room.

"Dad, why don't you join me in the back garden. It's a warm day. The sun will do us both good."

Didar glanced up from the TV, in his usual dazed state. To Omar's surprise, he nodded and rose from the couch, grabbing the arm to steady himself.

"What can I get you to drink? Sparkling water?" Again, Didar nodded as he shuffled to the back door. Omar's eyes met his mom's as he poured himself a beer and grabbed the Perrier from the fridge. Before he headed outside, she flashed an encouraging smile. He perched on a chair across the patio table from Didar and slid the Perrier to him.

Didar gazed through him. "The peonies are about ready to bloom." Didar wiped the condensation off his can of Perrier and shook the droplets off his hand to the ground.

"They're early, aren't they?" Omar tried to keep the conversation going even though he didn't have a clue which flowers were peonies.

"What day is it?" Didar cocked his head in Omar's direction. A cloud shrouded his eyes. It hadn't occurred to Omar his dad had lost track of time.

"Thursday."

"No, no. What day, month?" His voice cut through the air with the precision of a sharp knife. As much as the anger in Didar's voice caused a childhood shudder, any emotion beat the monotone syllables he'd been speaking for weeks.

"Uh, it's June 13." Omar took a sip of his beer keeping his eyes on his dad. Didar fell silent, his can of water sitting in a pool of condensation. Silence blanketed them. Then Didar mumbled something so quietly Omar almost missed it.

"Justice comes in many forms. It doesn't just happen in court."

Omar pushed his beer aside and leaned forward. His heart beat in his ears. "What do you mean by that Dad?"

Didar shook his head, eyes widening as he met Omar's stare, then he averted his gaze and scratched something stuck to the table top. "Oh, nothing, nothing. Just thinking out loud." He paused before continuing. "It's up to each of us to figure out where truth lies." He took a long slow swallow of water, his eyes fixed again on Omar. Water dripped off the bottom of the can to the table.

"What do you mean where truth lies?" The last mouthful of beer bubbled up to the back of Omar's throat. He swallowed to push it back down.

Didar sat in silence, clearing his throat before continuing. "You remember how I've told you over the years to be a good person? To pay it forward instead of paying backward like I've had to do?" He leaned forward, catching Omar's eye. "To think of those less fortunate and give your time and money? How it's not enough to say you appreciate those you love, but remember to show them how much they mean to you?" Didar sunk back into his chair.

Omar nodded. Those things entered his thoughts several times over the past few months. When everyone around him seemed to be walking away, those life lessons kept him by his dad's side.

"Well, I've been thinking about how all my attempts to turn my life around were me trying to prove to others I'm worthy. That somehow, they can judge me better. That I can erase my faults by painting over them." Didar paused. Omar tried to understand where all this was going.

"But somehow my past keeps bleeding through the paint and judgement doesn't change." Didar took another sip of water, giving his words time to sink in.

"But Dad, they found you not guilty. They judged you." Omar's brows knit as he tried to understand.

Didar slammed the can down on the table and leaned forward. "No, there was no judgement. The jury decided the prosecution hadn't proven guilt, not that I wasn't guilty. And the press, the public, they've judged me harshly regardless of the verdict. So, after all I've done to be judged for the man I've become, instead of for the man I once was, is for nothing." Didar paused and took a deep breath and leaned back. "But in the end, it's clear to me the only judgement I need is from you."

Omar's breath quickened. All the doubts sitting in his periphery came into focus. The flowers, the charity, the lessons about lying were stitches sewn by his dad to mend past deeds. The woman in the bar throwing a drink in his dad's face and his quick forgiveness. It all made sense. The very presence of Jahana. Proof of something more than his dad would admit. The dead, raped woman; pushed to the back of Didar's mind on purpose? Or forgotten because of a drunken stupor? His dad unable to admit the possibility he could be responsible. And now, he wanted him to judge him? Tell him he was a good man?

Omar stared at Didar slumped in the chair across from him seeking his judgement. Before the trial he would have assured him, he was a good man. Maybe even a great man.

But as he sat in silence heavy with expectation, it dawned on Omar, he needed to stop seeking the truth. Truth was secondary to caring for the man who raised him. He loved and accepted the person sitting across the table from him. How could he judge his father?

Would it hurt to lie and tell his dad he believed him? That he was a good man? That he wasn't a rapist or murderer? But his dad taught him not to lie, unless necessary. Was it necessary now? A lie might help his dad move on. Omar would never resolve his dad's past. The best he hoped for was to move forward, live for the future.

Omar reached out and touched his father's hand. A tear caught in the corner of his dad's eye, held in place by a sagging lower eyelid. Expectation reflected in his eye. He knew the words Didar wanted him to say.

Omar rose from the table, put a hand under his dad's elbow, encouraging him to stand. "Come on Dad, let's take a closer look at those peonies."

ABOUT THE AUTHOR

Heather Dawn Gray is a creative writer with a long career in laboratory medicine. After 25 years in healthcare she obtained her Master of Arts in Communications and Technology, formalizing 40 years of dabbling in fiction and non-fiction. Four novel writing courses led by David Allan Hamilton, culminated in the publication of her first novel, a realistic contemporary genealogical fiction, and prequel to this novel, '*The Lie*'.

Canada is proudly the country Heather identifies as home, but Australia also holds a place in her heart. She has visited several other countries, drawing inspiration from people and places along the way.

It was her own DNA test in 2018 that revealed surprises and led her to question 'What if…' resulting in the birth of her first two fiction novels.

Heather and her soulmate, Ron, have two daughters, Sabra and Colby, who are pursuing their professional careers in Alberta Canada and Queensland Australia.

Feel free to contact the author through her contact page on her website https://heatherdawngray.com/. Honest book reviews on Amazon and Goodreads are appreciated.

Manufactured by Amazon.ca
Bolton, ON